THE
LAND
TAMERS

**Center Point
Large Print**

**This Large Print Book carries the
Seal of Approval of N.A.V.H.**

THE
LAND
TAMERS

STEPHEN BLY

CENTER POINT PUBLISHING
THORNDIKE, MAINE

This Center Point Large Print edition is published in the year 2009 by arrangement with the author.

The text of this Large Print edition is unabridged. In other aspects, this book may vary from the original edition. Printed in the United States of America. Set in 16-point Times New Roman type.

ISBN: 978-1-60285-339-3

Library of Congress Cataloging-in-Publication Data

Bly, Stephen A., 1944-
  The land tamers / Stephen Bly.
    p. cm.
  ISBN 978-1-60285-339-3 (alk. paper)
  1. Large type books. I. Title.

PS3552.L93L36 2009
813'.54--dc22

2008031935

To Theodore Wilson
who left me more than he knew

CHAPTER
1

"No trees." Sandy stared out the window and shook his head. "This country wouldn't be half so boring if they'd plant some trees," Sandy mumbled to himself.

High society would have looked at this man and called him *gaunt*. But out west the word was *hardened*.

The Union Pacific train rattled along somewhere between Omaha and Cheyenne. Sandy wasn't sure just where he was. To the south he could still see the winding path of the North Platte. To the north stretched the vast prairie of the newly formed state of Nebraska. Straight ahead, two thin lines of cold steel melted together and plunged into the western horizon. Behind him, the East. All that Sandy ever knew existed back there. Too much sorrow. Too much disappointment. Too much trouble with the law. He made a habit of forgetting, but now and then the memories stole back.

The war lost, family scattered or dead, hope harder to find than a whisper on a windy day. He felt the uncomfortable rush of old feelings and quickly looked for a diversion. For the hundredth time his eyes focused on the weathered sign posted at the front of the railway car:

May 10th, 1869, Great Event. Railroad from the Atlantic to the Pacific, Grand Opening of the Union Pacific Railroad. Platte Valley Route. Passenger trains leave Omaha on the arrival of trains from the East. Through to San Francisco in less than Four Days, avoiding the Dangers of the Sea! Travelers for Pleasure, Health, or Business will find a Trip over the Rocky Mountains Healthy and Pleasant. Luxurious cars and eating houses on the Union Pacific Railroad.

"That was a year ago," Sandy commented to himself, "but things haven't changed much." When he purchased his "One Continuous Emigrant Passage" in Omaha, the agent told him $111 would get him to San Francisco in four days, four hours, and forty minutes. Give or take. Give or take Indians, buffalo, unseasonal storms, mechanical failures, and train delays.

Stale air permeated the train car. Smells of unwashed bodies, cigar smoke, and home-cooked food tucked away in baskets mingled with strong perfume, reminding Sandy of New Orleans' Canal Street about sundown any day in August.

Sandy slumped in the seat, leaning his right shoulder against the wall of the car, and yanked his brown hat down across his eyes. This signaled others he didn't want to be disturbed, but didn't block his vision. He was on the lookout, always on the lookout. As usual, he relaxed his whole body, except his eyes and his right hand. Whenever he entered any room or train car, he automatically plotted his defense, offense, and escape route. He would rest, but he wouldn't sleep.

Sandy rarely slept in daylight. At night he tossed and turned, except under the stars. That was home, since 1862, the year he marched out of Winchester, Virginia, to join Colonel Blackhaven and the Confederate army.

"Just a show of force and they'll change their position," Blackhaven had promised the Shenandoah volunteers. "Lincoln doesn't have the heart to see this through."

As the hot prairie sun soothed his neck and shoulder, Sandy allowed his thoughts to drift a moment. He had fought in about every Southern state. "The Shenandoah Stinger" they called him. Blackhaven knew a crack shot when he saw one. Some folks bragged that Sandy Thompson could shoot the eyes out of a squirrel at three hundred yards. Sandy indulged in a rare smile. That just wasn't true. Many a squirrel lost its life with eyes fully intact.

As a precision marksman, Sandy rode wherever the Confederates needed him. But even the few times it seemed they might win, Sandy hated the war. He treasured peace and solitude too much. And now that he knew how to shoot men instead of game, he didn't enjoy the changes in himself.

Even before the war he dreamed of moving to the frontier. The simple life.

He grew up on the war. He learned how to read horse signs, glance at the heavens and find his bearings, live off snake meat if he had to, and, thanks to the Baldwin brothers of San Angelo, Texas, he could outdraw anyone east of the Mississippi.

But he wasn't east of the Mississippi. That was one reason why his right hand now pressed against the polished cherry wood of his Colt.

"Mister! Mister!" The insistent voice was young, but Sandy responded with a partial draw.

A large stern-faced woman in a soiled blue dress clutched the boy in overalls to her side. She strongly resembled a mother hen huddling her chicks.

Sandy searched for an explanation. "Sorry, son, I'm really tired and you startled me. Now, what did you say?" He pulled out a bandana and wiped off the back of his neck, then pulled off his hat and mopped his forehead.

The boy glanced up at his mother and she loosened her grip. He broke into excited chatter. "I was tellin' ya 'bout that funny-lookin' storm." He pointed past Sandy through the window. "You don't 'spose it's a tornado, do ya?"

Sandy peered north. He placed his hat to the back of his head and surveyed the horizon. A huge tumbling wall of brownish clouds rolled across the prairie toward the train. Other passengers crowded to the windows and strained for a look as the train began to slow down. In a moment the conductor appeared.

"Dust storm?" Sandy asked.

"Worse," came the gravelly reply. "Buffalo. Now, remember, folks, them is wild animals. Nobody, absolutely nobody, get off this train until they pass through."

Sandy shoved down his window. He and the boy stuck their heads out for a better view. The roll like distant thunder intensified. They had to shout to be heard. Now they could see the dark brown hides of the stampeding herd. The ground under the buffalo quaked, and the rail cars clattered like rocks in a tin can. The boy grabbed Sandy's arm and pulled him down. He yelled in his ear. "They ain't goin' to run us over, are they?"

Sandy shook his head, but he really didn't know for sure. If those animals chose to come straight for the train, there wouldn't be anything left but splinters and grease spots.

At that moment the main point of the herd bulleted straight toward the train's engine. Those in the lead slowed their onslaught for just a split second. It proved fateful. The wild runners just behind them didn't slow a bit. Buffalo trampled buffalo. Cows squalled and bones crushed. Most of the passengers jerked away from the sight.

Sandy continued to stare, mesmerized. *Trampling the very leaders they followed,* he mused. Somehow it reminded him of Vicksburg, or maybe Little Elizabeth Creek.

A massive press of downed buffaloes served as a shield to divert the stampede around the train. Sandy chanced to remember his engraved pocket watch. He pulled it out of his green satchel and timed the advance. One hour and thirty minutes later, the last buffalo stormed past. Everyone in the car cheered and applauded. Some ran to the door to view the fallen animals up close. Dirt flew everywhere and tinted clothes, skin, and train alike. Each passenger gasped to find a clean pocket of air to breathe. They coughed, spat, and begged for drinks.

Sandy stepped outside the car and whipped the dirt from his trousers. He pulled out his pistol and spun the chamber, then quickly replaced it, making a mental note to clean it before dark. Some rifle fire from the east caught his attention. He found a couple of elderly men finishing off the wounded buffalo that bellowed in misery.

"How many head?" he asked the shorter man, who wore a tattered buckskin jacket.

"I reckon about a hundred." He lay bead on another animal, and his Henry rifle completed the sentence.

"No, I mean, in the stampede. How many would you guess?" Sandy interjected.

"Well, son, I don't know. I'd guess five . . . no, maybe eight or ten thousand head. What would you say, Danny?" The other man ignored the question and kept firing.

As the air cleared, women shook out blankets and clothes. The conductor corralled some passengers to the south side of the train. "If I can get two or three men to rustle up some firewood down at those cottonwoods, we'll get a fire raging and let you try some roasted buffalo. There's not a sweeter meat around."

A party mood swept the crowd. Men searched for wood, and women dug into the provisions for a real prairie nooner. The old man in buckskin grabbed Sandy's arm. "Say, son, you want to make ten dollars?"

"What can I do for you?"

"Grab my extra knife and help me and Danny skin these animals. The hides is worth money. But there's no wagon to haul them off, and the buzzards and coyotes'll be on them soon. Whatever we skin we can toss on the train and carry to the water station. Me and Danny can peg them out up there. What do you say?"

"Beats carrying firewood." Sandy braced himself for a messy project.

Sandy didn't need the ten dollars that much, nor did he relish blood and guts work. But he liked learning new trades. He had never skinned a buffalo before, and it looked like he'd learn from some of the best.

By the third animal, Sandy had the swing of it.

And by the time the passengers settled down to roast buffalo, Sandy, Danny, and old Nate were half-through. Sandy peeled off his shirt, tossed it up on the open train car window, grabbed a swig of water, and returned to the carcasses.

Sandy stood a tad over six feet without his boots. He hadn't been still long enough the past several years to put on any fat. The veins locked tight on hardened muscles as he rolled over another big bull. Sandy's grainy blond hair set off his hard, tanned skin. The quick glance of his steel gray eyes caused many a girl to take a step closer and many a brawler to pace back. With his back and chest exposed, the scar that traced his belly from one side and clear up to his shoulder blades was obvious. Being from the old school, neither Nate nor Danny asked about it.

In the West you knew only as much as a man chose to reveal. The past was his own. Sandy appreciated that. The West was the great equalizer. It mattered little whether you'd been a lawyer, a dentist, a storekeeper, a major, or an outlaw. You might come from high society or might have walked off the streets. Your brother could be a senator or a preacher. A dozen servants could have dressed you, or you made your way west barefoot. If you could ride all day, shoot straight, keep to yourself, work hard, laugh a little, and above all, keep calm in times of danger, you found respect.

The conductor called out for everyone to load up just as Sandy tugged the last hide on top the car. In a little over three hours they had skinned seventy-four buffalo and saved twenty-three heads for mounting. The other hides were too mangled to save. The passengers watched the vultures begin their slow, spiraled descent.

"I'll swan, Nate," the conductor chuckled, "you got those things piled as high as Chimney Rock. How far you goint to take them?"

"Just out of stink range," the old-timer roared as he cinched down a rope on the fresh hides.

Sandy cleaned up the best he could. He shook out his shirt again, buttoned the sleeves, and investigated a red stain on the right cuff. *Guess it's time to get a new shirt.* He sighed. He tied his bandana around his neck and climbed aboard.

He accepted an offer of meat from the little boy and his mother. A little darker than beef, the buffalo tasted about the same. Sandy devoured it as he sat across from Nate and Danny, who delighted each other and the passengers around them with buffalo stories. Sandy listened as he cleaned his Colt.

Danny finished with this one. "Yessir, I was up in the Dakotas back in '58, kickin' around them cricks, lookin' for color. Ain't nothin' up there. No use lookin', 'cept maybe on Injun land. But there ain't enough gold in the whole world to get me to go in there. Anyhow, bein' a young fool, I wanted

15

to keep lookin', so I 'cides to build a little cabin and sit out the winter. So many buffs wanderin' around a man couldn't starve if he wanted to. Why, you could just go out with a knife and fork and ask them to roll over.

"Now, wood is a might scarce up there, so I made me a dugout. You know, the bottom half down in the dirt, and the top part wood. I found me the nicest little hill and plopped her down right on top. Ain't much at carpenterin', but I can build a chimney. So I builds me the biggest, fanciest one you'd ever see. Good thing I did, too. Why, it saved my life.

"In the fall, right after the first snow, the buffs started movin' into the territory by the hundreds, then the thousands. I wasn't huntin' 'em back then. 'Sides, I didn't have a string to haul 'em out on. Well, one day I go to open the door and a huge bull is leanin' right again' it. I couldn't even open the blamed door. I got my rifle to drop the critter, but realized in time that if he died on the spot, my door would still be jammed.

"I didn't put no window in that shack, since I didn't want to look at no Dakota winter, so I was trapped in my own cabin. I took my axe and chopped a hole in the side of a wall over my bunk, the whole time hatin' to bust up that wood. Stickin' my bean out the side of the cabin, all I could see anywhere was them crazy buffs. I mean, they was packed in for miles. I could see my old cayuse picketed down where I left him, but there was solid buffalo between me and him.

"I didn't dare shoot my way out, 'cause they could stampede on me. I figured I'd just have to wait it out. But about then, that old bull at the door got impatient with my hospitality. He just invites himself on in. The leather hinges on the door gave way and he waltzes in with a friend or two. I start shooin' them with the butt of my rifle, but they don't take kindly to the action. Instead, they bellow out for the whole gang to come a-callin'. I'll swear, two dozen of them critters filed into that tiny cabin and would'a pushed the walls down, 'cept for it being dug out in the ground.

"I thought about climbin' onto the rafters, but feared I couldn't hold on long. So I kick the coals out of the fireplace, pour the water out of the kettle on the coals, and climb into he kettle so's I can stick my head up that big chimney. The way them buffs leaned against the kettle I'd a been crushed to death, if it weren't fer it bein' cast iron, and the good job of buildin' that smokestack.

"There I was, feelin' like a durn fool, lookin' up at the blue sky, and gettin' fresh air through the stack. I felt like Jonah in the belly of the whale. I was about ready to pledge myself to be a preacher, if the good Lord would see fit to rescue me, when he thought better of the offer and decided to get me out another way. Them coals I kicked out of the fireplace hadn't really gone out, and they scattered some. My bunk and table, bein' already crushed by them buffs and layin' in pieces on the sod, caught fire. As the smoke and flames got more powerful, the critters panicked. Rather than waitin' for someone to hold open the door, they just crashed through the walls at any place they chose, leapin' up above the sod as they fled. The result bein' that in a matter of seconds my cabin lay like a pile of smoulderin' toothpicks in a hole in the ground.

"I see that the smoke backed them buffs clear past the trees and my horse. I carefully sneak out of the rubble and over to my gray geldin'. I have to mount up Injun style, since my saddle's trampled to shreds, along with the rest of my worldly goods.

"Well, that old hoss proved his worth by threadin' us out of that massive herd, with me havin' nothin' but the shirt on my back and one round in my rifle. As we passed through 'em, I discovered why they'd picked my place. Them big brown weed-eaters was a-lickin' the ground like it was candy. Danged if I hadn't gone and built my cabin smack-dab on top of their favorite salt lick. As it turns out, I was the intruder, not them. Anyhows, if you ever get up that way—and if you got any sense you won't—ask where Chimney Lick is, and you'll see one of the finest fireplaces north of the Missouri."

Nate and Danny paid Sandy in silver and got off

the train at a wood-and-water siding. Sandy dozed off and on, dreaming about buffalo, until the train once again pulled to a stop.

Cheyenne, Wyoming Territory, wide-open and wild in the summer of 1870. The Kansas Pacific Railroad just completed its line, joining Denver to Cheyenne, and the town blustered as the staging point for renewed interest in the Colorado gold mines. Law was hard to find. Order didn't exist. In the past three months Cheyenne wore out five town marshals. Two were gunned down. Two were chased out. One left on the same train that brought him in.

As Sandy Thompson debarked for a dinner break, he quickly noted two types of people. Eager Easterners with a little money tried to find a way to strike it rich in the West. Hardened Westerners, both male and female, worked to find a way to relieve the Easterners of their money. Hotels, saloons, and makeshift tent-covered casinos lined the streets.

Sandy observed it all. "Watchin' folks is an education," his daddy used to tell him. And Sandy was a graduate student. He played his old game of "What would I do if I were they?" as he walked along.

He stuck his head into a place called The Dirty Cat. A poker game was in progress. Ever since spending six months in the war in the same outfit as Freddie LaBou, the riverboat gambler, Sandy enjoyed watching others play the game. But he seldomed anted in himself. The sheer entertainment and show of false bravado amused him.

The dealer, a big man with full gray beard, had most of the winnings piled in front of him. But he looked nervous. Several men around the table routinely bet, called, and dropped. Meanwhile, a man across from the dealer, clad in buckskin and long flowing hair, showed signs of agitation.

In the West there was no one way a man had to look. The way you acted was always more important. The man in buckskin sported a drooping handlebar mustache that twitched noticeably as he lost another bundle on jacks and queens. He stomped away toward Sandy and shook his head in disgust. "It's just not my night. Have you ever seen the luck? I'd better quit while I'm behind."

Sandy tossed his head at the dealer. "Well, it's not my game," he said, "but if it were me, I'd send someone down the street for a new deck of cards."

The dealer jumped to his feet. "You sayin' I'm cheatin' at cards!"

Sandy looked the big man over slowly. "All I'm saying is, if I were the man in buckskins, I'd send out for a new deck. Those seem to be a tad worn-out, at one end, anyway."

The man in buckskins wheeled around. "Shaved?"

Sandy turned toward the door, purposely showing his back to the gaming table.

"Turn around here and draw!" the dealer

shouted. "Nobody questions my integrity and walks away!"

"*I* question it." With lightning speed the man in buckskin whipped out his gun only inches from the dealer's midsection.

The heavy stomach heaved up and down. "You made a big mistake, mister, pointing a gun at Big John Dreary."

"No, you made the mistake, shoving shaved cards on Bill Hickok. I think we've got a few more hands to play out . . . with a different deck." The force of his pistol on the dealer's paunch backed him into his chair.

"Thanks, stranger, I'm obliged." Hickok nodded to Sandy. With gun still in place, he took a coin from the top of the dealer's stack and flipped it to Sandy. "Dinner's on me."

Sandy left The Dirty Cat and sauntered toward the Granite Hotel. Some claimed the back wall of the Granite, the oldest building in Cheyenne, was built by Jim Bridger himself. Although burned down twice, it had been rebuilt, larger and fancier each time. The legend of activities in the upper rooms of the Granite spread through the plains faster than a prairie fire.

Sandy studied the fairly new whitewash that had already begun to flake off the front porch. The Wyoming sun baked it right off. He scraped his boots on the second step and pushed through the door.

He ate his dinner alone and spent the time with assorted thoughts of his family. For all his failures, he appreciated the two things drummed into him years before. Daddy always said that the thin line between gambling and greed couldn't be trusted, and Momma told them that strong drink robbed more lives than all the thieves in history. Sandy couldn't help but smile at the remembrance.

The best way he handled grief was to try to forget it. But every once in awhile a voice, or a glance, or a dream, or even the aroma of home-baked apple pie transported him back. Sandy, Ralph Wayne, and Darlene riding along the river, diving off Big Sandy Bluff, hunting squirrels and pretending they were bears, camping in the woods while Daddy and Uncle Henry chopped trees. Sandy ached for the old familiar slap on the back, the hearty laugh, or the sight of the strong calloused hands.

"Mind if I borrow a corner of your table? I'm in a hurry." Sandy jerked up as a short man removed a black bowler and sat down.

"Oh, sure, it's all yours. I'm about through, anyway. I guess it's pretty crowded in here."

"A zoo, that's what it is, a blamed zoo! But I love it." The newcomer poured salt on his stew and speared a hunk of beef with his knife.

"You love crowds?" Sandy asked.

The man wiped his hand on his shirt and held

out his hand. "Harvey Sheets is my name. I run the Dry Creek Outfitters up the street. Crowds mean business is booming. Only problem is keeping help. They get twenty dollars in their pocket and head to the gold fields. Me and Molly been running the store all alone for almost two weeks. Say, you aren't looking for a job by chance?"

"Afraid not. I'm headed to California." Sandy pushed his pie plate to the center of the small table, leaned back in his chair, and stretched his arms.

"It used to be simple," Harvey rambled on as he shoveled knifeloads of beef into his mouth. "You just geared up a few mountain men, sold supplies to the big cattle outfits, and traded a little with the Indians. Nowadays, they're lined up six yards deep ready to buy everything in the store. Not only that, but every hard luck case east of Omaha wants to buy on jawbone credit, or just steal you blind."

Sheets waved to several men sitting across from them. "That train has made a world of difference to this country. 'Course I'm not sure it's all been good. Why, you can't trust folks anymore. In the old days a man like No-Neck Mowrey would come in, pick up a few hundred dollars worth of goods on credit, and you'd know you'd get paid back in the spring, no matter how hard the winter. Why, back in '61, No-Neck rode three hundred fifty miles out of the way to pay me my due . . . three hundred fifty miles! Some of these characters won't walk across the street to do the same. Things are changing, all right . . . things are changing."

Sandy nodded his head in agreement and pulled on his hat.

"If you ever get up Montana way, look up old No-Neck. There's no finer man in those mountains," Harvey Sheets called out as Sandy walked away.

Ever since he'd crossed the Mississippi, somebody was always telling No-Neck Mowrey stories. No-Neck and the grizzlies. No-Neck and the Crow Indians. No-Neck and the Dry Gulch disaster. Sandy wondered whether such a man really existed.

He parked himself on a depot bench and waited for time to reload the train. Looking over the mass of human confusion, he sorted through some passengers boarding a Denver-bound train. Several men wore army uniforms. By nature, Sandy shied away from blue uniforms. Too many years of wearing the gray, too many worries about a certain lumber mill robbery in Virginia.

Across the depot he spotted a sergeant pushing his way past an Indian woman to grab the arm of a blond, bearded fellow about to board the train. Sandy couldn't hear the conversation, but a shoving match ended with the sergeant punching the bearded man hard. Something about the stance of the sergeant and the bearded man's look of pain flashed a flood of scenes to Sandy. The torment and cruelty of Fort Edwards . . . an insane commanding officer. . . .

The call rang out to load up on the westbound. Sandy quickly climbed up the steps and flopped down into a scuffed, olive green seat. He hoped to have the whole seat to himself, some peace, some quiet, some room to stretch out. He got his wish. By the time the train lurched out, the unshaven, buffalo-smelling drifter sat quite alone.

Sandy, the observer of people, watched several passengers for amusement. He studied their movements, their words, their expressions. He was always assessing, judging, even projecting, but seldom did he commit himself to a person. He had his own agenda. He had his own world to conquer, and he left others to their own.

Sandy didn't consider himself antisocial. Not at all. Just independent. Reserved. Uncomplicated. "That's it," he assured himself, as he witnessed the last light of day on the vast Wyoming prairie. "I just like things simple."

So the West beckoned him. It was wide open, primitive, untouched by mass civilization or war. Sandy, like countless others, viewed the West as a place to start over. To get back to important things. Back to basic values. Back to open, honest dealings. Back to faith in something.

Others heading west sought great wealth, huge

estates, or political power. It would be enough for Sandy Thompson just to find a peaceful spread to work.

For a long time he drank in the changing shadows of the Wyoming prairie. Then, at last, some sleep.

CHAPTER
2

"Ain't that some sight?"

The hot July sun slowly burned through Sandy's beard stubble as the train crested the mountain for a winding descent. A column of steam hung in the air as the cars plowed through it. The red-barked cedar and tall ponderosa pines blurred as the train gained speed.

"I said, 'Ain't that some sight?' Come on! You can't sleep all day!"

Sandy stretched his stiff arms and legs, massaged his neck, and looked around in irritation. "You talking to me?" He now had a seatmate. After one glance at him, Sandy squinted through the window. Over the pines and across a rocky bluff he could make out the Great Salt Lake Basin of Utah Territory. Straight ahead a lake spread as wide as an ocean. The train had paralleled the old Mormon trail most the day, and now it forked north at the mountains.

"It must have been in the spring when they first came," Sandy muttered under his breath. "Surely no one would choose this burned-out land in the heat of summer."

"Won't be no time at all we'll be in Ogden," the man next to him said.

Thompson wasn't sure what was most repugnant about the man. Maybe it was the two shining gold teeth in an otherwise toothless grin. Perhaps it was the greasy, crumb-filled red beard, or the stench.

"You been sleepin' since I got on at Rock Springs," he announced, and offered Sandy some chewing tobacco.

Sandy declined and tried to ignore the man. He looked around the train to see other new passengers. Several drummers, a couple with six children, an army sergeant visiting with a young Indian woman who wore the latest Eastern fashions. Sandy untied his red bandana and wiped at his forehead.

"I seen them boots. You a Union man?" his seatmate asked.

Sandy tensed. "Those are Union boots, aren't they?" he replied.

The red-bearded man spit in the general direction of a brass spittoon. "Shoot, I wore Union boots for three years and I ain't been east of Cheyenne since '45. You can buy them off any outfitter. I got a pair still on my shelves. My question stands. Did you fight Union?"

"Who wants to know?"

"Just conversation, son. Just conversation." He picked up an old black leather satchel and pointed to faded words on the side: Mudd City Mercantile, C. E. Mudd, Prop.

"You own a store?" Sandy ventured.

"Store? I own the whole town!"

Sandy made a mental note never to come within twenty miles of Mudd City. Mudd continued in a near whisper, "Don't worry, son, out here it don't matter much whether you was Union or Rebel. I suspect you was from the South, since they're the ones to keep it hid the most."

Sandy relaxed a bit. He slid down in the seat and tried to straighten his long legs ahead of him. "I'm not ashamed of it. Grew up in the Shenandoah Valley. Winchester's home grounds. Not too much left there now."

"Winchester? Never heard of it. Who won?"

"We won twice, lost twice. Doesn't matter now."

"So you're comin' out west to make your fortune, right?"

"What I'm doing here's my own business."

"I seen your kind, lots of times. They file through here by the hundreds, always lookin' to make a strike. Maybe I can help you."

"I just need some breathing room, thank you."

"Where you headin'? You got a destination, don't you?"

28

"Angel Camp, California. Got some kin there. A sister, and her husband."

"Well, it's too late for California."

"What?"

"I say, it's too late. Gold's dryin' up. Nothin' left but Chinamen and squatters."

"I didn't say I was looking for gold."

"Oh, I know, a sister. Heard that before, too. I say a man comes west to find color, or to get away from the law. You in trouble, son?"

"Listen, Mudd, or whoever you are—" Sandy felt his neck muscles twitch.

"You can call me Montana. Everybody else does."

"You must be kidding? Montana Mudd? Anyway, I didn't get on this train for the purpose of discussing my personal affairs with some foul-smelling, gold-toothed windbag!"

That silenced Mudd. But his mention of the law still struck a nerve. Sandy breathed hard on the window that reflected the flashing landscape. Past scenes reeled by, too: Standing near General Kerby Smith at New Orleans when they knew they had to call it quits. A year of riding back to Virginia through the Union-occupied South. The day he rode into Winchester, summer of '66 . . . carpetbaggers everywhere, his mother dead, the family mill sold. He protested about the mill to the authorities, but got nowhere.

In '67 he rode south to talk to Mr. Jefferson Davis, who awaited trial at Fort Monroe. No help there. Last fall he took revenge. He broke into the mill office and uncovered two thousand dollars in the safe. He took just twelve hundred dollars of it and left a note: *Paid in full.* That was the amount they got for the mill at the auction.

Sandy sighed. *So now I'm a thief, a wanted man.* He suddenly got homesick for Darlene, his sister and only living relative. He hadn't seen her since '61. Nine years was a long time. She could be anywhere by now. But the only lead he had was Angel Camp. Half the twelve hundred dollars was hers. He intended to see that she got it.

A voice jarred him to the present. "Come on, son, it's time to get off."

"I'm going on. Good-bye, Mudd."

"You ain't goin' for about four hours. The train's got to stock up. And you gotta eat and change cars. Grab your gear. We can eat at Tweedy's."

Sandy determined to eat anywhere but Tweedy's. He eased his six-foot frame into the aisle and lagged behind in the back of the car until the passengers filed out.

The army sergeant picked up the Indian woman's luggage. She asked for it back. When the sergeant insisted on carrying it, Sandy heard a curt "Get lost!" The stunned man sat down and watched her storm off. He caught Thompson's smile. Their eyes froze for a moment. Somehow, Sandy felt they had crossed paths before.

A rush of war images returned. Broken bodies,

blood, men crying in pain, the praying. . . . Why would one glance at a rebuffed army sergeant touch off all this, Sandy wondered.

"Don't that beat all?" the sergeant whined. "Send 'em back east to school and they think they're better than you."

Sandy spoke slowly now, biting off each word so that the hearer wouldn't misunderstand. "Maybe she *is* better."

The sergeant whipped around to eyeball Sandy again. The veins on his neck began to bulge and glow in anger. "What did you say?"

"You heard me. Seems to me she—"

"There's no squaw alive better than me, and that includes Miss Sarah Winnemucca." The sergeant looked like he expected Sandy to fight.

Instead, Sandy yawned. "Well, my daddy always said if you want to impress a lady, you've got to act like a gentleman."

The frustrated soldier flexed to land a punch. But he hesitated. Maybe it was Sandy's broad shoulders and strong hands. Maybe it was the revolver on his hip. Maybe it was the look in the eyes that said, "I can take you anytime, any place." Maybe it was something else. The sergeant tramped out of the car without a word.

Winnemucca? Sandy mused. He'd heard that name before. Piute chief, or was it Modoc? During the trip he'd heard lots of Indian stories. It was hard to remember one from another.

31

Sandy stepped onto the depot platform with a quick look around. Only a boy and a dog sat on a stack of boxes and barrels. The barefoot youth was eating an apple. Sandy tossed his duffle bag down on a bench with a pile of others and glanced down Washington Street.

"Where's a good place to eat?" he asked the boy.

His face lit up. "You rich?"

"Not hardly, but I do want a good steak."

"Then go anywhere except Michner's Hotel. They'll make you eat off a white tablecloth. Try Patty's Palace down on the other side of the court-house. But sometimes it's kind of wild." He smiled a toothy grin. "I mean, that's what I hear. I ain't never been there."

Sandy thanked him and strolled down the street. He half-expected to see the sergeant. When there was no sign of him, he took time to notice the paradox of this area. A hot stinging wind rolled into Ogden off the Salt Lake Basin, yet mud stood in the streets. A sudden summer squall must have hit during the night. The water reflected the silhouettes of the varied skyline of the buildings. The hotel, a new two-story brick building, freshly painted, displayed a long covered veranda and sidewalk. Right next to it huddled a wood clapboard unpainted boardinghouse with false front, no sidewalk, and an old dead cottonwood out front. Sandy noticed Tweedy's down from there, packed with train passengers.

He glanced through some dry goods that sat on a barrel outside the People's Emporium Cooperative Store. A smartly styled bib-front shirt caught his attention, but the color, navy blue, wasn't right. He walked past what he was sure were Ogden's finer homes. Two-story frame buildings with outside stairs leading to top floors seemed to be the pattern. *I guess that's how they keep their wives from fighting,* Sandy thought.

He turned west and crossed the tracks. Several blocks further the plaid-shirted Virginian swung open the doors to Prairie Patty's Porterhouse Palace. Sandy paused to adjust his eyes in the dim light. A rough voice hollered, "Hey, son, over here. I saved a place for you."

Sandy groaned as he spotted the red hair and shining teeth. "I thought you were going to Tweedy's, Mudd."

"Too crowded. Besides, I didn't know my good friend, Patty, had opened this fine establishment. Ain't this a coincidence? Must be fate."

An auburn-haired woman in a bright red dress walked up to take their order. "Patty! This here is . . . say, son, what is your name?"

"Thompson. Sandy Thompson, ma'am. I'd like a big steak and keep it bleeding."

Patty shot him a brief nod. "Sure, Thompson, I know just what you mean. How about you, Montana?"

"Same as the kid here."

"He doesn't look like a kid to me," she said with a smile. Mudd winked at Sandy.

Patty rustled off in her taffeta as Mudd leaned closer. "Listen, Thompson, ain't no use you goin' to California. It's all washed up. Better to go to Montana or the Idaho territories. Why, there's Virginia City and Last Chance Gulch and Idaho City, just to name a few. And don't forget Silver City and Pierce. That's where the action is. Now, tell you what I'll do, bein's we're friends. . . . Come on up to Mudd City and I'll outfit you at a fifteen percent discount. You can't beat that. Got some savings, right? You ain't busted, are you?"

"Mudd, I'm not busted, but I have a mind to cram that candle up your nose until the hot air in your head explodes. What I have is none of your—"

A voice from behind broke into Sandy's tirade. "Mudd! Get those hands above the table! One sudden move and you're a dead man!"

Sandy stared into two rifles and a drawn pistol. Four men flanked their table. He felt like a fool letting his disgust with Mudd prevent his seeing this trap. Sandy edged out of his chair.

"Hey, you! Sit down, and keep those hands high."

"Look," Sandy protested, "you've got some beef with Mudd, so you solve it. I just want to eat my steak."

"Yeah, let my partner go. You got no quarrel with him."

Mudd's words startled Sandy. He glared at Mudd as one of the gunmen inspected him all over. He pulled Sandy's gun out of the holster. Another pushed a carbine just inches from his head. "Now, if you two will kindly step outside. . . ."

Sandy smashed against Mudd as they were both shoved out the door.

"Where's our thousand dollars, Mudd?" one of them demanded.

"Now, boys, let me explain. You know them hides weren't yours, and when Louie showed up claiming them, I had nothin' left to sell."

"Mudd! You can't lie your way out of this one. A deal's a deal. One thousand bucks for those hides. What you did with them later is your business, not ours. You ain't leavin' town until you've paid, or you ain't leavin' town . . . ever. Understand?"

"You guys sure messed things up. I was just concluding a lucrative transaction with Thompson here. You could have had your money by dark. But now that you've bushwhacked us right in the middle of negotiations, I can't say what Thompson'll do."

"Mudd, cut it out," Sandy hissed. "I've got nothing to do with you, so leave me out of it."

"See? What did I tell you, fellas? You blew it. There goes your money."

The man with the pistol thrust the two toward a side alley about two feet wide. "In that case, Mudd. . . ."

Suddenly Mudd propelled Sandy into the others. They fell back like dominoes. Mudd fled to some buildings in back of the alley. One of the men jumped up and fired after him. Sandy landed a hard right to the stomach of the gunman nearest him and grabbed his rifle. He scrambled toward the street and dove behind a barrel as more shots rang out. Then he darted into some shadows. As he turned the corner, he stopped for a quick look around and a frantic glance toward the depot. An unexpected movement from Prairie Patty's doorway forced him back a step into the alley. That was the last he knew as pain ground into the back of his head.

When he came to, the sun had long been down. Faint moonlight outlined the building wall that formed his resting place. His head throbbed. He felt along the ground and through his clothes. He'd been stripped. No gun, no money pouch, and he'd missed his train.

He struggled to sit up. As he leaned against the building, he took stock of his situation. How in the world could he go out to dinner and end up in such a mess? He couldn't pull his hand away from the piercing lump on the back of his head.

He regretted losing the money more than any-thing. But then he had to admit he hadn't felt comfortable about the coins since he took them. He reasoned to himself that it really belonged to him, since the mill had been stolen. He wanted to believe he had only taken his fair share, but it didn't sit square deep inside.

Maybe this is God's way of doing justice, he thought. *They stole from me. I stole it back. Now, who knows who has the money?*

All he wanted was to get back on the train headed to California, to get to Darlene. Then, he remembered Mudd. "Mudd! Montana Mudd!"

He swayed to his feet and searched for a storefront that resembled a sheriff's office. He doubted that anyone west of the Rockies had heard of a mill robbery in Virginia. At least, he hoped so. With clenched fist he banged on a likely door. "Open up! I need to talk to a sheriff."

A short squatty man peered through the slightly cracked door. "The sheriff's gone. Chasing a killer. Come back tomorrow."

Sandy felt nauseous. "But I've been robbed."

"What's the matter? One of the women roll you?"

"No, I'm on my way to California. Got off the train to eat at Prairie Patty's. These men jumped us with guns, pulled us out in the alley. The next thing I know I'm unconscious in the dirt and cleaned out."

The man swung open the door and ushered Sandy in. "I know all about it. Your first mistake, mister, was not eatin' down at Tweedy's or Michner's Hotel. No tellin' what can happen to a stranger when you wander down into those badlands." The plump man played with his jailer's badge, then squinted at him. "You know a man called Montana Mudd?"

"I wish I'd never heard the name. He sat beside me on the train and he was at that restaurant when. . . ."

The jailer backed up to his desk and pulled open a drawer. He slowly drew out a pistol. "This here your gun?"

Sandy jumped forward.

"Stay right where you are. No funny stuff." The jailer pointed the Colt at Sandy.

"Sure, it's my gun. Where'd you get it?"

"We think somebody shot old man Emory with it. Sheriff's at Emory's place right now. The old man got all his horses stolen, too. So you're under arrest. At least, until the sheriff gets back."

"Look, you need to find those men who yanked us out of Prairie Patty's. They had some beef with Mudd. Since I had the misfortune of sitting at the same table, they dragged me along. Go ask Patty. There were plenty of witnesses. It's obvious I didn't shoot anyone, or why would I be here. Look at this crazy lump on my head. I've been unconscious for hours! You can't hold me."

"Sure can. As soon as it's daybreak, the sheriff's heading out with a posse to catch up with your partner, Mudd. He's the last person seen leavin' the livery stable where Emory got a hole through him."

Sandy rambled on to make conversation while his eyes darted around the candlelit room. The old survival instinct began to well up inside him. That old instinct had kept him alive when many others faltered and fell. "But I never even knew Mudd before today. Why would I come busting into your office if I'd just shot someone?"

"I'll admit it sounds pretty dumb to me. But I ain't takin' no chances. Now, if you'll just back up right over there to the jail cell. . . ."

Sandy slowly turned around. As the jailer jiggled his keys, Sandy kicked the iron bars against the man's hand. The jailer dropped Sandy's pistol and the keys on the wooden floor. Sandy punched him twice in the middle and once in the jaw. The man fell. Sandy grabbed his .44 and ran into the night.

He found a saddled horse tied to a post in front of Prairie Patty's. He untied it and led it to Patty's back door. He banged as loud as he dared. He heard a soft noise inside. "Who is it?"

"Please open up. I need to talk to Patty."

"We're closed. Come back tomorrow."

"It'll just take a minute."

"Sleep it off, cowboy. I'm not opening this place for some drunken buckaroo in the middle of the night."

Sandy kicked the door handle and the interior bolt ripped away from the rotting wood. The door flew open to a café kitchen. Patty stood in a blue flannel nightgown, a meat cleaver in one hand. Her red hair was pulled back and tied behind her head.

"Oh, it's you! But if you think I won't use this, then you aren't half as smart as I thought you were. Why haven't you and Mudd left town by now? Everyone's looking for you."

"I have no idea where Mudd is. I've got to find him. Is that your horse outside?" Sandy looked out of the room as they talked.

"No, it's been around here ever since you two left this afternoon. I reckon it belongs to one of those guys chasing after Mudd."

"In that case, you won't mind my borrowing it. Someone stole every penny I have to my name. I've got to get it back." He looked her over as a thought flashed. "Say, how come you let me lie out there next to your building all afternoon. You in on this?"

"Listen, mister, there are two-bit drifters like you lying in the street every day. Besides, I didn't know you were there. All the action's been down at the stable." She clutched the meat cleaver tight as ever.

"Can you tell me which direction to Mudd City?"

"Mudd City? That's a new one on me. Are you sure there's such a place?"

"I'm not sure of anything. Where's this guy Mudd from?"

"Who knows? He talks about Big Springs, Henry's Fork, places like that." She pulled her robe tighter as the east wind drifted through the moonlit doorway. "I suppose he's from up that way. But you can't believe him for much."

"Where's Big Springs?"

"About halfway to Virginia City, Montana, on the west side of the Tetons. It'll take a good week of ridin' to get there. But then, lookin' for Mudd will be like huntin' for a mouse in a buffalo herd."

Sandy tried to contain his agitation. Then he thought of a plan. "Down at the station on the back bench is an old green duffle bag. It's mine. You can get it in the morning. Nothing in it much but a few clothes and some pictures. Rolled up in a red bandana is a gold pocket watch. It's worth at least twenty-five dollars. You can have it if you'll give me some food and supplies. I can't chance going down there myself."

"You expect me to believe you? A crazy man who busted in my door?" But Sandy thought he detected a relenting in her voice.

"What choice do you have?"

She raised her eyebrows. "I could scream."

"And I could shoot you. In this part of town, who'd notice?" It was more of a challenge than a threat.

"OK, it's a draw. Get your grub and get out. If

there's a gold watch down there, I won't report you. If there isn't, you'll have a dozen new charges hangin' on your head."

Thompson grabbed a flour sack and moved toward the cupboards. Patty directed his search from across the room, cleaver still in hand. "Take that jerky, some flour, the beans are in the barrel. Don't forget those dried apples. But remember, only one at a time. They swell right up in your stomach. They could bust your gut if you eat too many."

"Well, thanks. Sorry—"

"Sorry! You wake me up, break down my door, and take my food. . . ." Patty dropped the cleaver down to her side. "Be careful, y'hear?"

Sandy backed out with his bag and led the gentle black horse to the north side of town. He couldn't hear a sound anywhere. As he mounted, he wondered if the animal could survive a week's hard riding.

And he did mean to ride hard for as long as it took to find Mudd and his money. The thought never occurred to Sandy that he wouldn't find them. The old survival instinct took over again. He didn't quit easily. Truth was, he never quit.

CHAPTER
3

In July, any trail in the West is dusty. With the breeze, the basin turned to a miserable dirt bowl. Sandy Thompson railed at the wind and stopped near a creek at noon to wash and get a drink. The whirlwinds of soil flying everywhere blocked his view of the Wasatch Mountains, and the howl of the wind muffled the trickle of the stream.

As he rested, he had sense enough to realize this dust storm favored him. If the Ogden sheriff followed him, he had a built-in smokescreen for the clouds of dust he stirred. No tracks to trace, either.

What little he ate that day he chewed from the back of the saddle. Jerky and dirt. Bread and dirt. Dried apples and dirt. He tried not to press the black horse beyond his endurance. At times the horse seemed to sense directions better than Sandy.

Sandy felt at a disadvantage. His usually keen vision and ability to plan strategy at a glance kept him one step ahead of potential tangles. But this swirling mass out of northern Utah had taken away that leverage. He rode with pistol tucked in his trousers, away from the elements, but inches from his grip.

Time seemed to stop as he jostled along. No

familiar guideposts marked his progress. Each mile looked like the last, and the next. The horse settled into a medium gait. He appeared experienced at long rides.

The elements didn't become still until late evening. By mutual consent, man and beast quit for the day in a meadow beside a small creek. Thick brush lined the creek, and the rushing water tumbled down steep granite banks and crashed to pools below. Here the roar of the falls dominated the air.

Sandy pulled the worn leather saddle from the black gelding and rubbed him down with a couple handfuls of leaves. With the bridle still in place, Sandy led the horse to the creek for a drink. He guarded the approach from behind the whole time. The noise of the waters could hide anyone who neared.

He splashed water on the horse's head, brushed it off with his hands, then led him back to the small meadow. He had just hobbled the horse when he spied a rider with a string of horses on the hill opposite the creek. *A trapper or buffalo hunter with a winter's gleanings,* Sandy surmised.

"Got room in that meadow for some hungry critters?" the man on the lead horse shouted across. "I hoped to make camp here tonight. Didn't expect to have company".

"Sure, why not?" Sandy hollered back. It wasn't until the whole line crossed the creek that he noticed the girl, an Indian. She rode the last pack-horse. As the older man pulled off hides, the girl made camp and prepared a meal.

Sandy offered to aid the man. He needn't have bothered. Massive muscles rippled in the arms of the gray-bearded, weather-beaten hunter. His head hunched low to his neck. His chin appeared even with his shoulder blades.

Then Sandy caught the motion. "Don't move!"

The old man dropped his last bundle and let out a war cry. He yanked his knife out of its sheath and sliced the air. Sandy stared at a three-foot snake lying in pieces on the ground. He also spotted the two bloody fang marks on the back of the grizzled man's wrist.

"Timber rattler," the man muttered. He just stood there, as though stunned.

Years of swamp fighting had trained Sandy well. He wrenched off his belt and cinched it down on the hairy arm. He jerked the knife out and warned, "This'll hurt."

Sandy lacerated the wound, sucked the blood and poison out, and spit it on the ground. Moments later the men took stock. "I think we got it," Sandy reported.

"If I'm still alive by morning, I owe you. Must be getting senile. It's been a long time since a snake beat me out."

The man squatted and grubbed up a small shrub with tubular roots.

"That a potato?" Sandy inquired.

"Not quite. It's called a camas plant." He cut off a few roots, sliced them lengthwise, placed them on the wound, and wrapped them with his bandana. "They'll suck some more on that poison," he explained as he flopped down next to the fire.

Sandy unloaded the rest of the hides and picketed the string of horses across the meadow. Sandy noticed that the girl never said a word during the whole ordeal. Her face expressed worry, however.

"Where you coming from?" the man asked.

"Ogden. But, I'm from back east. It's a long story. I just got off the train at Ogden."

"Imagine that. You can ride a train clear to California. Times change fast. You heading up to Bear Lake?"

"No, I'm trying to reach Big Springs or Henry's Fork. You heard of them?"

"Sure, but you can't get there down this trail. You're aimed straight for those Cache Mountains and right down to Bear Lake. I just came from there. You should have veered left at the cottonwoods."

"I couldn't even see the fork in that storm."

"Well, you're just a few miles off. Besides, it's better to camp here. I'm sure glad you did. I can't figure how No-Neck Mowrey could freeze like that."

Sandy looked up, startled. "You're No-Neck Mowrey?"

"Yep, one and the same."

"Do you know a man in Cheyenne named Sheets who runs a hardware store?"

"Harvey Sheets? Known him for years. He's a good man. Staked me through two bad winters in a row. Not many like him left around."

Sandy laughed. "He said the same about you. He told me if I ever got to Montana to look you up." Sandy reached out his hand. "By the way, I'm Sandy Thompson."

Sandy saw the Indian girl look him over. She kept on watching his every movement. Fry bread sizzled in her skillet.

"Glad to meet you, Sandy," No-Neck said. "What part of Virginia you from?"

"Now, how'd you know I was from Virginia?"

"I left Lynchburg in '34. I don't ever forget a Virginia accent. Lost mine in these mountains. But hearing you sure brings back a lot."

"I'm from the Shenandoah."

"Harper's Ferry?"

"No, Winchester."

"I hear the war ripped that up pretty good."

"You heard right."

The girl drew closer. Her face screwed up tight as though to unscramble the words. "Too bad," No-Neck continued. "A beautiful place. I rode west on a horse I bought in Edinburg. You'll have to fill me in on what's happening back there." He called to the girl, "You got some Arbuckle's ready yet?"

"Soon, soon," she answered. Her voice had a sweet ring.

No-Neck turned to Thompson. "If you're serious about riding to Henry's Fork, why don't you tag along with us? We've got to make it for the Mud Flats Rendezvous. That's where the companies come to pick up winter hides. We trade them smelly buffalo rugs and a few good pelts for our year's supplies. Ain't what it used to be. About played out nowadays."

Sandy smelled fresh meat frying as No-Neck said, "I spend the fall south of Bozeman. Then, I head up the Yellowstone. I move to Jackson Hole for the winter. Everyone else moves out . . . claims it's too harsh. That gives me a good start on spring. I trail off to Bear River for a few fresh pelts before the rendezvous. Been at it almost twenty-five years now."

"Who's the girl?" Sandy inquired. "Isn't she too young for a squaw?" The girl covered a laugh with her hand.

The old man roared. "Mowrey is seventeen years old. That isn't too young for anything. But she's not my squaw. She's my daughter. Her mother was the hardest working woman I ever met, rest her soul. We were hitched up for fourteen years."

"What happened to her?"

"Blackfoots shot her. They were trying to steal my hides about three years ago, fifty miles north of the great falls of the Missouri. It was my fault. I never should have strayed that far into Blackfoot country." The old man paused a moment and drank down some coffee the girl handed him.

"Mainly greed," he reminisced. "We'd been following elk sign for about six days. It looked like a huge herd, and I have this hankering for elk jerky. My Elaina could spice up jerky like no one ever. . . . Anyway, I kept pushing up into Blackfoot territory, thinking any day now we'd catch up. About daylight I lit out to take a look for them elk and left Elaina in camp. I hadn't been gone more than an hour when I caught up with the elk. I snuck around on the east side of them, so they wouldn't smell me, and crawled in close as I could.

"I could have shot one easy, but I wanted two or more, so I crawled up to about thirty yards short of a big buck. I brought him down, but the whole herd bolted right toward me. I was so worried about turning the stampede that I forgot to bring down another. Instead, I just fired wildly in the air with my pistol. I turned them all right, but in the process the whole herd panicked and ran over the top of my kill. There was so little left of him I had to abandon trying to dress him out.

"I spent a couple hours trying to catch up with them again, but I didn't have any luck. So I headed back to camp. What I didn't know was my shots attracted a party of young Blackfoot bucks looking for trouble. They planned to haul off all my goods and my Elaina too. Only they didn't know her.

"They got my gear, but they sure didn't get Elaina. When I got there she was holed up against a dirt bank. Shot up good, but still breathing. Told me she had killed two of them. I figured they'd come back with help, so I patched her up the best I could, built a travois, and headed south. She didn't make it to nightfall. Anyway, I hauled her all the way to Madison and gave her a proper burial. She was a good woman. It was her bad fortune to get hooked up to an old skunk like me. So now, it's just me and Mowrey."

"Mowrey? Is that your daughter? Doesn't she have a first name?"

"That's all we ever called her. Never had a son, so I guess that's the best way to keep the family name going."

The long-haired girl brought them both another tin of coffee. The boiling liquid stung Thompson's tongue, and stuck in his throat. As he gagged, No-Neck snickered and Mowrey grinned. "Come on," the old man chided, "you'll never make it out west until you can handle mountain coffee. I just take a pound of Arbuckle's, spit in it, and boil it until a spoon floats."

As No-Neck rambled on, Sandy watched the

Indian girl. Close up, she looked more mature. When she caught Sandy gazing at her, she pretended to ignore them both. She dished up their food. Sandy figured her to be about five feet tall. He calculated she weighed about a hundred pounds, no more. She was silent, yet self-confident, and Sandy bet she'd be as fierce as her mother in a battle.

After dinner No-Neck checked his string while Sandy gathered more firewood. The sky faded from deep dark blue to black. Sandy loved the outdoors at this time of day.

The three of them huddled around the fire, not so much to keep warm, but to listen closely to the stories. At first, No-Neck did most of the talking. He pulled out a slightly worn ivory-bowled pipe and lit it. "I left home in '34. But it was early in '36 before I made it to the Rockies. Things were different then. Took a lot longer. I even stayed a couple days with old man Clark in Missouri."

"Clark? You mean, William Clark? You knew him?"

"Didn't know him well, but I did spend a night or two talking with him about the West. His health wasn't all that good, but, my, how he liked to talk about Indians and mountains and grizzlies. He was a fine old gentleman. Died just a few years later, so I hear."

No-Neck Mowrey sighed deeply. "I've seen a lot of changes in this country. Most of them's been bad." He laid his head back on his saddle. "Used to be if you treated the world square, you'd get along fine out here. You treat the Indians square, the companies square, the other trappers square, and the animals square. . . ." No-Neck yawned as his last words dropped. "But nowadays . . . oh, heck, that's the way all old men talk, isn't it?"

Sandy told his story. He even mentioned the money from the mill and his trouble in Ogden. For the first time, sitting with a man like No-Neck Mowrey, he felt comfortable spilling out these things.

"So you ran into Clarence Earl Mudd, better known as Montana?"

"You know him?"

"I buy rotgut from him every July. He's got a little hole-in-the-wall up at Mud Flats."

"Would that by any chance be Mudd City?"

"Yep, that's what he calls the place. And it's true it's got plenty of mud."

"Is he a merchant?"

"Of sorts. Most of the time he's selling junk and some whiskey. It keeps him alive, I guess. If you're in a hurry to settle your score with him, you could head out on your own. But you could stumble into that sheriff. If you wait, and proceed slowly with me, I promise to get you to Mudd's place by rendezvous time. He won't be any trouble to you. He never wears a gun, you know."

"But he must have had one down in Ogden.

Somebody got shot up at the livery stable. They claim he did it."

"Wasn't Mudd, I know that for sure. Must have been one of those fellows after him."

"How can you be so certain?"

"Mudd's never been the shooting type. He'll cheat you, all right, if you let him. You get him mad enough, and he'll pull that long knife out of his boot. But he won't shoot. Been with him plenty of times. We've faced Bannocks and Piutes, even once fought against some Mexican soldiers. He even refused to shoot one of those murdering Blackfeet. Some men are just that way. He says it's against his religion to carry a gun. What do you think, Thompson, does the Good Book say you can't carry a gun?"

"Well, I'm no expert, but I don't see much difference between David's slingshot and our Winchesters, except a few centuries. It seems to me the Lord doesn't care much what you carry, but he cares a whole bunch about who you bring down. I guess every man's got his own opinion on the subject."

No-Neck slurped on another cup of mountain coffee. "I can tell you one thing—Mudd's about the only man I've found out in the country that can survive more than a day and a half without a gun. Maybe he's got the right idea. He'll probably outlive us all."

Sandy slapped his leg. "If he thinks he can take

off with my money, he shortened his lifespan a whole lot."

They snacked on some of Sandy's dried apples and then settled in for the night. Sandy's bedroll had to be shaken out, but it was dry and warm. He crawled under the rough wool blanket and watched Mowrey adjust her blankets over by the horses.

Sandy stared up at the stars. The creek sounded closer in the stillness. An occasional crack and pop from the fire punctuated the water's roar. He searched through the stars for the big red one in the south. When he found it he traced the outline of Hercules. They stood out so much clearer in the western sky, Sandy thought. "Everything seems clearer," he said softly.

For the first time in many months he slept well.

Sandy woke to the smell of steaming beans and the sight of Mowrey flitting around the fire. Cold bread and hot coffee completed their breakfast. As they ate, Mowrey whispered something to her father. "Mowrey here wants to know if she can have another of those dried apples. She really liked them."

Sandy tossed her one, and the dark-haired beauty smiled at him for the first time. Their eyes met briefly. Something about that fleeting glance made Sandy feel good. He stayed cheered up all morning. It must have been the combination of the good sleep, the hot food, the pleasant day, the satisfying visit with No-Neck Mowrey, and, of course, the sparkle in a pretty lady's eye. Strange, the subtle changes of the past few hours.

No-Neck showed off his arm. "See this? No swelling. Just a little pain. This man saved my life, Mowrey. Tell you what, Thompson, you help me get these hides up to Mud Flats and I'll provide the chuck. That is, Mowrey will do the cooking for us."

Sandy liked the idea. As he looked at No-Neck, he could tell Mowrey awaited his reaction as well. "I've got nothing to lose. If Mudd's going to be up there all summer, I guess another day won't hurt."

About seven o'clock they started out. Some dust began to blow again, but No-Neck guided them. "This is like the time me and Elaina were up on the Judith," he jawed as they rode along. "It was about September, and we were low on meat when I spotted tracks of a griz among the huckleberries. We followed those tracks back to the river and spotted him there in the brush. He stood a good nine feet. I knew it'd take both of us to bring him down.

"So, Elaina hung little Mowrey up in a tree and loaded my old single shot .50 caliber Springfield. The plan was simple. Elaina was to fire the first shot. Then, when the bear turned toward us, I would finish him. Well, I mean to tell you, Elaina's mark hit him right below the left ear. He turned and started toward us, blood pouring down his face something fierce.

"I took careful aim and squeezed off a round. I hit him right in the Adam's apple. Most animals would have had their heads blowed off by then. But this old yellow-haired devil kept right on after us. I tried to squeeze off another round, but the trigger stuck. By now, we could see the anger in his eyes. I hollered for Elaina to grab the baby, I threw a handful of dirt at the griz and hauled off for the river.

"If you've never seen a bear run, you'd be surprised how fast they can travel. I'm sure he wasn't ten feet behind me when we got to a cliff overlooking the Judith. I didn't hesitate to dive over that cliff. Neither did the bear. He jumped right in after me. I hadn't hit water before a shot rang out. Elaina had put another slug in him. Caught the big guy in the lungs as he hit the water. Poor old griz drowned about three feet from where I was treading water. Talk about heavy! Don't ever try dragging a wet grizzly out over a steep riverbank."

Mowrey interrupted. "Speaking of all wet, it's time we heated some water for you two and me." She jumped off her mount.

No-Neck laughed. "That's her way of saying we'd better get ourselves cleaned up. This is a good place as any to stop."

Sandy stripped to the waist and used his bandana for washing. It wasn't exactly a bath, but at least he could eat without having to bite into dirt.

No-Neck kept asking questions about Virginia. He avoided any direct questions about Sandy's involvement in the war. The moon shone bright and full, Mowrey slept soundly, and the fire glowed only coals before the discussion stopped. "I don't really miss it at all," No-Neck concluded. "I just miss having someone to talk to about it. That's the only drawback to life out here. Sometimes you gotta talk. Me and the horses have had many a lonely conversation. If the danger don't make you a praying man, then the loneliness will."

About noon the next day the dust storm completely subsided. No-Neck announced they'd entered Idaho Territory. Sandy spied some riders in the distance. "Indians?"

"Not likely. Not enough game down here. Probably that posse of yours. This could get a little tight. Quick! Do what I tell you. Mowrey, fix Thompson, here, like a squaw, and hurry!"

Mowrey spoke directly to Sandy. "We'll have to trade horses."

"What?"

"You get on the squaw horse and take off those boots."

"Do what she says," No-Neck prodded, "unless you want to go back to Ogden."

Sandy hopped on the last packhorse and pulled off his boots. Mowrey giggled at the white skin shining below the grimy ankles. "You're a mighty pale squaw," she teased. She took off her long moccasins and gave them to Sandy. "Hurry, roll up your pant legs." Mowrey covered him with her Hudson's Bay company blanket. Nothing showed but his face and moccasined feet. "Whatever you do, don't look up," she warned. "Look away and down. They expect that from a squaw, and they won't be suspicious." Mowrey rode off to the right on Sandy's horse.

When the riders approached the slow-moving pack, No-Neck directed them to the side of the trail. Sandy had his .44 cocked under the robe.

"You got two squaws now, No-Neck?"

"Not hardly, Sheriff. That's my daughter over there. You remember Mowrey, don't you?"

"Don't guess I've seen her in years. She grew right up, didn't she?"

"They all do."

"Why's she riding way over there? She isn't hiding something, is she?"

Thompson tensed.

"I hope to heaven she's hiding something," No-Neck bantered back. "I hope she's hiding that odor! Went out to gather wood last night and tangled with not one, but two, skunks. Even a senile buffalo wouldn't come close."

"Have you seen anybody coming through?"

"Haven't come on to nobody since the Bear Lake Trail. How many you looking for?"

"Don't know for sure. Four, maybe five. Big Curly Celter, his brother, Brad. Probably Pat Hawker and T. Walters. And a stranger, a blond-headed Reb. Anyway, hate to go back, but we got to."

"You calling it quits, Sheriff Stanton?" No-Neck inquired.

"Can't go no farther. I've got no jurisdiction past here. You headed for the rendezvous?"

"Where else, with all these hides?"

"If you see Mudd, you tell him to get himself back to Ogden. He's mixed up in this somehow."

"Montana don't take orders from no one, especially once he gets holed up. You know that," No-Neck declared.

"He'd better this time. Mudd was the last one out of a stable before some shooting started. Someday we'll get some law up here in this territory, and I won't have to make these long drives north."

No-Neck snorted. "If they get law up here, we'll have to move the rendezvous."

One of the posse members suddenly pointed toward Sandy. "Hey, would you look at what's on that last pony?"

Sandy froze again.

"Where'd you get them good beaver pelts, No-Neck?" the man demanded.

"Now, I'm not about to confess that to anyone. There's not enough up there for even one."

Sandy slowly breathed out. As they passed by the posse he tried hard to keep a straight face. The trick had worked. The men did not know that the moccasined, blanket-covered "squaw" on the last horse in No-Neck's caravan was really the blond Rebel they were seeking.

Far down the road, No-Neck stopped the pack. He let out a whoop. "What did I tell you? Mudd's no killer. He left town before the man got shot."

"Maybe so," Sandy conceded as he threw off the buffalo shawl, "but he's still got some explaining to do. He's got to know what happened to my money."

"If I were you, I'd worry more about Celter and his gang. They're a real mean group," No-Neck cautioned.

"Mowrey," Sandy called, "how about giving me back my boots and horse?"

Mowrey rode in close. "Too bad they didn't stay for dinner," she said with a grin. "The new squaw could have cooked it!"

CHAPTER
4

"You a Shoshone?" Sandy asked Mowrey as they sauntered down the trail.

"No, Nez Percé." Mowrey brushed back her hair from around her eyes.

No-Neck turned around. "She's got folks up at Wallowa Lake. But she's never been there. I met her mother up on the Clearwater. There's a missionary station up there. We had a real church wedding. Can you imagine that?"

"No fooling? A missionary station?" Sandy sounded surprised. Somehow the country didn't seem like the kind of place where ministers would be easy to find. "So Mowrey's been on the trail all her life?"

"Nope. Sent her off to an Indian school for several years. But when my wife died, well, it just worked out for her to come along. I'm getting too old to go it alone."

The next few hours found Sandy realigning his thinking about mountain men. The rumors had circulated around the east coast for as long as he could remember about the hardened men and the wild times. It seemed incredible to Sandy that here was a man who, some twenty years ago, had a church wedding and a long marriage. *Obviously, here is a man of principle,* Sandy thought.

The mountains to the east had blocked the direct sunlight for most of the morning, but the wide-open prairie to the west had just the opposite effect in the evening. The sun reddened as it started its final descent. It seemed to Sandy to hang up there a long time, stretching shadows and slowly cooling down the air.

Just before sunset, the winds died down. As they

reached the northern mountain range, the trail twisted parallel to the mountains. Occasional stands of pine, fir, and cottonwood shaded the travelers, and, more critically, darkened the campsite toward which they were headed. No-Neck hoped they could reach it before it got any darker.

What they didn't know was that the campsite was occupied.

Leaning against a scraggly pine was Big Curly Celter.

"There ain't no reason to follow Mudd any further. He's getting up into rendezvous country. I'm not about to take on that pack of mountain men. We'll settle our score some other day. Can't head south. We just barely outran that posse as it was. Besides, T. left a man dying in Ogden. I say we go for Virginia City."

"I tell you, Curly, it's different up there now. They've got vigilantes. Pat and I got run out last fall. I ain't going back. What do you say we try Silver City and the Owyhees?"

"I'd rather spend winter in Bozeman," Pat Hawker broke in. "I got some kin up there."

"Well, winter is a long way off and I don't plan on spending it broke. Maybe we ought to swing out around the Salt Lake and head down toward Arizona Territory. I hear there's some silver towns that are wide open. If we run some luck, we could clean up and spend the winter in Denver. Now there's a town to get stranded in," Big Curly suggested.

T. Walters kicked a pinecone down toward a little creek and pushed his hat back. Thoughts of the notorious Arizona Territorial Prison made him shudder. "I ain't getting close to A.T.P. I hear they pay the Indians a dollar a head to bring back escaped prisoners—dead or alive. Besides, it's so hot down there even the lizards get blisters."

Big Curly stared in the distance, not really following T.'s comments. Then he spoke. "Hey, you boys see what I see?"

The men jumped to their feet.

"That the posse?"

"No way. Looks like a buffalo hunter's string."

Pat Hawker grinned. "Well, now, things aren't so bleak after all."

T. glanced at Curly. "Are we going to relieve them of their burden?"

"It's the least we can do," Curly said. "How many down there?"

"Three. But one looks like a squaw."

"She'll run to the hills when the shooting starts. So that means two guns."

"It's tougher than that, Curly. Look who's leading the string." Hawker was standing on a granite rock, shading his eyes and looking down the trail.

"No-Neck! Aw, we can take him. Just don't let him get that Sharps pointed in your direction.

There won't be enough left of you to put in an envelope to mail home. T., you and Hawker crawl behind those rocks by the clearing. Keep down until they pass you. We'll stop them up front." Curly barked the commands.

Pat Hawker hesitated. "Do we got to kill them? Can't we just take off with their gear?"

"You leave No-Neck for a witness and we won't be safe anywhere west of St. Louis. We either go all the way or sit it out right here. Remember what happened when we left Louie LaFever?"

T. pushed Hawker forward. "Come on Pat, I don't plan on freezing my tail off in some line shack all winter. Let's get going."

Sandy Thompson breathed a long sigh of relief. His luck was definitely changing. No sheriff chasing him. He'd soon demand restitution from Mudd. In the meantime, he rode beside a Western legend and an attractive young lady. Now he remembered why he had headed west. He wanted country that was open, free, uncluttered, a place where a man could do some serious thinking, planning, dreaming.

This country's not all that bad, he thought to himself. *A man could run cattle along these foothills in the winter and find a mountain valley for summer grazing. Why, you could plant a few fruit trees along the creek, and. . . .* Sandy rode into a clearing among the trees and rocks. He stopped and stood up in the saddle to survey the mountainside. "This would be a good spot for a cabin," he commented to No-Neck. "Perfect view of anyone coming up the trail."

The first crack of rifle fire echoed through the still woods. Startled, Sandy and Mowrey dove from their horses. No-Neck tumbled off. The first bullet had hit its mark, and the long-barreled Sharps fell with him.

Sandy didn't have time to regret his normally unfailing concentration. He leaped into rote action. Bloody Southern battlefields had driven fear from him long ago. Even Mowrey moved with lightning speed. She grabbed No-Neck's cartridge belt from the back of his horse and pulled her father to cover. Then the horses bolted. Hawker and T. crawled up from the south while Curly and Brad Celter tossed lead from the north.

"How bad you hit, No-Neck?" Sandy yelled between fire.

"It's bad, real bad, but I'm alive."

"Can you see who it is?" Sandy surveyed the rocks and trees staring down the sights of his .44.

"I ain't in a mood to ask. Bushwhackers, I suppose. Now, save those shots. Make them count. Wait for them to make some mistakes."

Sandy blinked in amazement. That's what General Jackson always told them: "Hold back till they make some mistakes."

Hawker was the first. He gambled a move

across the trail for a better angle. He never made it. Sandy's bullet spraddled him in clear view.

"That helps the odds," hollered No-Neck.

A barrage of bullets from the north signaled a cover by Curly and Brad. Sandy moved close enough to see No-Neck bleeding profusely from the center of his massive chest. While Mowrey desperately tried to stop the flow, Sandy traded shots with T. to the south. Brad Celter raised up for a better aim.

Even in his state of shock, No-Neck could hit a careless gunman seventy yards away. The Sharps roared over the top of the slaps of the pistols and Brad Celter's lifeless body banged against the boulders. Meanwhile, from farther up the hill, Curly was moving in slowly toward the trio.

A hard-breathing No-Neck rasped out toward Sandy, "I can't . . . get no fire from . . . the other one. He's either . . . dead or up to something . . . look out for an ambush!"

No-Neck's instinct told him danger lurked nearby, but he couldn't see more than a few feet ahead. He shoved his Sharps toward Mowrey.

T. kept shooting, but he began to panic as he wondered why he didn't hear anything out of Curly. When he failed to draw Sandy out of the woods, he began to pull back for his horse, one tree at a time. Like any good soldier, Sandy knew what to do when the enemy was on the run. He quickly followed T.

Panic under fire does strange things to men. Sandy had seen it all before. T. Walters was so scared he actually threw down his gun and ran to catch his horse. Sandy had an open shot, a no-miss situation. He aimed the eight-inch, round-barreled Colt .44 army revolver. A routine procedure, a big target. Yet, this time, he couldn't do it. He'd had enough of shooting young men who fled from battle. The gunman mounted up and rode hard toward the south.

Sandy consoled himself with the thought that with any luck the fleeing gunman would stumble into the sheriff before the day was over. A rifle shot followed by a blast of the big Sharps buffalo gun startled Sandy's thoughts back to No-Neck's direction.

He found Mowrey leaning over No-Neck. At the base of the rock cliff, no more than fifty feet away, lay the body of Big Curly Celter. No-Neck gasped from a new wound. "I guess . . . he snuck up on the ridge . . . knew it was coming . . . nothing I could do . . . but he made his mistake . . . he should've shot Mowrey first."

"What?"

"She had the lead out of that Sharps before he had a chance to squeeze off another round. . . . She's the second-best shot in the West . . . since her mother died, that is."

"I'll round up the horses. We've got to get you some help."

Mowrey objected. "I'll get the horses. You'll take too long." She ran off without waiting for Sandy's reply.

"Let her go," said No-Neck weakly. "She's right . . . but don't matter. . . . There's no hurry."

"Look, I'll get rails and we'll make a sled for you. Maybe we can get you to a doctor." Sandy was searching for some hope.

"No such thing till Bozeman. . . . Save your strength. . . ." No-Neck closed his eyes.

Sandy pulled off his shirt and wadded it up, pressing it against the chest of the big trapper, trying to slow down the bleeding. The entire gunfight had lasted less than fifteen minutes. Sandy sighed as he thought about the speed at which life changes come. He lifted up No-Neck's head and propped a mossy rock underneath, hoping to improve the wounded man's breathing.

The old man tried to clear his throat to talk, but his voice could barely be heard. "Listen . . . careful there . . . got two favors . . . maybe three. . . . You and Mowrey . . . take the hides to the rendezvous . . . split the money. . . . Don't take less than fifteen hundred dollars . . . worth more. . . . Second, take Mowrey to that Indian school . . . Three Forks. . . . Maybe she'll amount to something. . . ."

No-Neck tried to raise up but made it to one elbow before collapsing back on the ground. "Listen to me . . . she's Indian, but she's my

68

daughter. . . . Don't go messing around with her unless you reckon to marry her. . . . So help me . . . I'll haunt you . . . I swear!"

The old man closed his eyes again, while Sandy watched helplessly. It wasn't the first time he had watched a friend die. But it never got easier.

No-Neck opened his eyes once more and stared up at the sky. He tried to reach around for Sandy. "Thompson? Thompson?"

Sandy gripped his hand.

"Other side of those spruce . . . a creek . . . Mink Creek it's called. . . . Bury me there, but don't mark the grave . . . country's too wild yet. . . . Someday . . . come back and dress me up a sign. . . . Put on it, No-Neck Mowrey, He Never Lost a Fight."

That was it.

No contortions. No gasping for breath. No pleas for life. No curses. No bitterness.

Just gone.

He was right, Sandy thought. *He never lost a fight.* In the summer of 1870, along a little-used trail in the Idaho Territory, No-Neck Mowrey died a winner.

Digging an adequate grave was a difficult task with no tools except the butt of a rifle and his own bare hands. But Sandy had done it before. Old memories die hard.

Chet Webster at Fort Royal.

Blake McMahon at Manassa Gap.

Captain Sid Westbrook at Sitlington's Hill.

Perry Boy Jones just outside New Orleans.

And Sandy's brother, Ralph Wayne, at Harper's Ferry.

Every time he had pledged that this would be the last he had to bury, but it never was. Sometimes Sandy Thompson dreamed of waking up buried in a shallow grave.

Working in the long shadows of twilight, he tossed the Sharps buffalo rifle in with the body of his friend. It was one of those times he wished he had something religious to say or at least a Bible to read. All he managed to say as he mounded the dirt and rock was, "Lord, he deserved better than this. How about you making up the difference?"

In a nearby pine he carved N. N. *Who knows?* he thought, *Maybe I'll make it back here and do a better job.*

Now his mind centered on Mowrey. She had been gone a long time. Did she just run off and leave him? He took his wadded-up shirt down to the creek and tried to wash out the blood and dirt. Even after wringing out all the water, it was freezing cold and wet when he put it back on.

A movement startled him. Pistol in hand, he investigated, only to find his own horse behind some deer brush. He readjusted the cinch and remembered the slain ambushers. With eyes scouting the woods for signs of Mowrey, Sandy led the horse back to where the bodies lay. He didn't relish the idea of looting the dead, but he did need the guns. He sure didn't want them used against him somewhere down the line. Somehow he was hoping to find his twelve hundred dollars on one of them.

Big Curley's rifle had busted in his fall from the cliff. Sandy gathered up Brad Celter's Colt .36 and slung it over his saddle. He never found T. Walter's discarded weapon, but what he discovered next to Pat Hawker was reward enough.

A .36 pistol in good condition lay there. A closer look revealed it to be a Ridgon and Ansley percussion revolver with polished brass trigger guard and handle strap still in place. The best thing about it, besides the extra ammunition, was the marking on the barrel: *Augusta, Ga. C.S.A.*

Sandy gripped the Confederate gun. He hadn't carried one since the war. He placed the coveted prize in his grub bag. He could not find more than ten dollars among all the men, so he left it in their pockets. It occurred to him that the man who fled might be the one who had his funds.

He went back over to where No-Neck had fallen and picked up Mowrey's tracks. The place was quiet and peaceful. Birds chirped, the creek gurgled, a soft breeze started up, then died, then started again. The sun continued its descent and a distant coyote howled. *Just like nothing happened,* Sandy thought. For nature, it was just the cycle of birth, life, and death. His mind now focused on the tracks in front of him.

Sandy followed Mowrey's trail about a mile up the mountain. He slowly walked his horse, cautious at every step. His mind searched for a reason why she was taking so long to return. Near the base of a granite rock slide he spotted what looked like other moccasin prints. Searching through the brush, he found tracks of unshod horses and a couple of pinecones that had been peeled down to their cores. There were, he knew, Indians nearby.

He figured that, whoever the Indians were, they had paused up here long enough to watch the whole battle down below. What about Mowrey? Had she been captured by them? Or had she run off with her own kind? Surely she wouldn't leave No-Neck in his condition.

Sandy had some tough choices. With less than an hour of daylight he could be a good ways up the trail. There was Mudd to catch, money to retrieve, and a sister somewhere to find. After all, he hadn't brought on this fight. *All I want to do is get out without any more complications. The simple life . . . somewhere there is a simple life.*

On the other hand, he could try his luck at following Indian signs and look for Mowrey. *But those Indians could be hostile. What if she joined them on purpose? They might just kill me for butting in.* Then Sandy remembered No-Neck's request. He wanted the hides sold and Mowrey taken to Three Forks. The thought of his promise to the dying trapper settled any debate he might have had going. He followed the tracks around the base of the rock slide.

He quickly realized that tracking light-footed, moccasin-clad Indian feet was a lot different from tracking a heavy-footed Union Army. A broken twig here, or a scuff in the dirt there, was all he had to go on. He held his Colt in his right hand and the reins of his horse in the left. Coming to a wide clearing, he crossed the creek and stood perfectly still against the evening shadows. He thought he heard a sound—a stick break, a rock clank, a pinecone drop, something. He waited for a long time without moving anything but his eyes, partly because he didn't want to give away his position, partly because he really wasn't sure what would be the best thing to do next.

If Sandy Thompson didn't know his next move, Nee-keah-peop did. Spotted Horse, as he was called by the Indian agent at Fort Hall, was the leader of the small band that had watched the fighting below. He and the others were returning from an off-reservation hunting trip when the sound of gunfire provoked cautious investigation. They found the packhorses milling down by the creek and quietly rounded them up even as the fight ensued. Then they had hidden themselves in the rocks and waited to see which side would win.

Spotted Horse had watched Mowrey wind her way up the same trail that Sandy was now taking.

But when she disappeared behind the granite rock slide, he knew that they had been sighted. With the pack animals tucked away in a little box canyon, Spotted Horse sent two of his men down the mountain to capture Mowrey and bring her into camp.

Growing up in the camp of one of the West's most notorious mountain men had prepared Mowrey for such a situation. She had no trouble staying out of the way of the first two braves. Her small frame and weight allowed her to scamper straight up the granite rock slide without making a sound or starting a minor avalanche. From the top she spotted the pack train in the little canyon corral, and, seeing only one guard, she proceeded down the hill with the intention of overpowering the guard with the impact of a granite rock. Her movement down the hill did not alert the Indians, but it did irritate another of the mountains' inhabitants. A fifty-pound marmot waddled out of its hole, squawked at Mowrey, and kicked a few stones down the hill.

Instantly two rifles were pointed in her direction, and there was no place on the granite slope to hide. She had no choice but to walk right into camp.

"Those packhorses belong to my father, No-Neck Mowrey," she announced.

"And where is your father?" Spotted Horse asked.

"He and the others down below are looking for me," she said, trying to bluff.

"Good," he said. "We will sit here and wait for them." He pushed her to the ground and climbed partially up on the rocks to get a view down the trail. Spotted Horse stood for a long time and saw no one coming up the trail.

"Perhaps it is time for us to go down and investigate this fight. It has been much time since any shots were fired. Maybe they have all killed each other!" The speaker was the tall brave that held a gun on Mowrey.

"Or perhaps they are waiting for us to move away from this hill," Spotted Horse replied.

He turned to Mowrey, who was staring at the pack train. "Maybe they have abandoned you."

"They will come," she said, confidently.

"And how many are there?" he asked.

"Many," she bluffed.

"No-Neck Mowrey travels only with his family. Why should I believe you?" His voice showed impatience.

"Nee-keah-peop, someone is coming, look!" a slender brave reported.

"Only one?"

"Yes, only one."

"Is it No-Neck?"

"No, he is too unsure of our trail. It looks like a younger man."

"Does he have yellow hair?" Mowrey asked.

Spotted Horse ignored Mowrey's question.

"He's coming after the girl," another brave instructed.

"Fool! He's coming after the hides. He won't care about the girl," Spotted Horse said, waving his arm in Mowrey's direction.

"What will we do?"

"Send him away empty-handed, that's what. Tie her up and stand guard. The rest of you, come with me. We'll give him a real Indian welcome."

CHAPTER
5

The first sight Sandy Thompson had of the Indians was the barrel of a rifle, just two feet behind his right shoulder. The battle ended without a single shot. The braves nearest Sandy yanked his .44 from the holster. They untied his rifle from the saddle and took the spare pistol that he had so recently draped over the saddle horn.

Spotted Horse spoke first. "You looking for something?"

Sandy was mad—mad at himself for walking into an ambush, mad at the fact that his life seemed to be sliding out of his control, and mad at some dirt-streaked Indians that held a gun at his head. There was a cool breeze tumbling down off the high mountains to the east, but Sandy didn't feel it. There was nothing condescending about his voice.

"You've got my pack train and hides and that girl. I want them back."

The rifle barrel behind him was now shoved sharply into the back of his neck. It was cold, but it didn't sound like the holder intended for it to remain cold for long.

Spotted Horse spoke with a composed directness. "Now, that's not the way I see it. Those buffalo hides came from animals on Bannock ground. We gave No-Neck permission to hunt and trap, but we don't know you at all."

"No-Neck's dead. He gave those hides to Mowrey and me."

Sandy searched for a way to duck out from under the pressure of the gun at his head. He was too tense to notice the tears streaked across Mowrey's face when he blurted the announcement about No-Neck's death.

"So, No-Neck's gone." Spotted Horse stepped around in front of Thompson. Both men were about the same size and the same build. From there on, all similiarity ceased. "He was a brave man. He's the last of the honest white men. But that doesn't change the facts. The hides belong to us now, and so does the girl."

Sandy waved his hand at Spotted Horse. "The girl's No-Neck's daughter. You can't just drag her off," he shouted.

Now it was Spotted Horse who got excited. "Listen, yellow hair, you've got no claims to anything. You are on Indian land. The hides are mine. The girl's Indian. That makes her mine, too. You whites have been dragging off our women for years. You got nothing, white man, but a gun in your back and a twitch of the finger from being dead." Spotted Horse slammed the butt of the rifle into Sandy's midsection. Sandy doubled in pain, reached for hidden strength, and started to throw a punch. The cold barrel of the rifle behind him jabbed into his right temple.

He changed tactics. "Look I've got no fight with you. Just give me back my guns, another horse for Mowrey, and enough hides to get supplies for a trip to Montana. We'll be out of your way in a flash."

"Who do you think you are talking to? You didn't hear me good. I said you get nothing. Tie him up."

They bound him next to Mowrey, then built a fire and set up camp. One brave skinned a small deer for their dinner. Three others reported back from a scouting party that all the whites had died or fled. One of them now wore a pair of boots that looked like Big Curly's. Another had on Brad Celter's pants. Sandy hated to think what they had done to the remains.

Mowrey managed a low whisper. "Is my father really dead?"

"Yes. I buried him down by the creek. Do you think they dug up the body?"

"No, I don't think they'd do that."

"Who are these men?"

"Bannocks, from Fort Hall," she whispered.

"Does that make them friends or enemies?" Sandy didn't look at Mowrey as he talked low. His eyes were on a constant search for a plan of escape.

"What does it look like? They're not as bad as the Blackfeet, but they are getting desperate. A Bannock up at the rendezvous last year said that the agent at Fort Hall is trying to starve them out."

"Where is Fort Hall?"

"About three days northwest. Those hides weren't taken anywhere near Bannock land."

Sandy noticed the tear stains that had now dried on Mowrey's cheeks. "Have they hurt you?" He looked into her eyes.

"No, not yet. Are you worried about me?" She managed half a smile.

"Of course I am. I promised your father that I'd get you back to Three Forks."

Mowrey glared. "I'm not going!"

"What? Do you want to stay with these characters?"

"Are those my only choices? I can never go back to the school in Three Forks. That school is just no good for me."

"Well, I made your dad a promise, and it's one I

plan to keep. You're going back to that school, provided we get out of this mess."

Spotted Horse brought them some meat and untied them just enough so they could eat. "In the morning, we're taking the girl and the hides to Fort Hall."

Mowrey started to complain. "Those hides aren't yours, and you know it."

Spotted Horse stared the girl into silence, but just for a moment. "What about him?" she demanded and waved at Sandy.

"We'll leave him tied to a tree. With any luck he'll be loose in a day or two."

Spotted Horse sat down, cross-legged, in front of Sandy. His rifle was across his lap as he ripped off a bite of deer meat. The other braves were busy with the horses, packs, and supper. Sandy lunged for the gun in Spotted Horse's lap. A sharp burn sliced into his left arm. He grabbed his arm and stared at the Indian's blood-covered knife. Sandy could feel his own hot blood pump through the fingers that were trying to stop the flow.

Spotted Horse jumped to his feet. He looked at Mowrey. "They are all dumb." He called for a couple of the braves. "Tie him up," he commanded.

"He'll bleed to death," Mowrey protested.

There are worse things," he said without smiling.

"Let me at least tie a bandage around his arm," she insisted.

"You talk too much." Spotted horse shook his fist at Mowrey. "You can bandage him all you want, but he stays tied up!" He walked away from the fire toward the horses and left Sandy and Mowrey in the care of a couple of the braves.

Mowrey dressed the wound as best she could. At last the bleeding stopped. Neither of them spoke. A very thin Indian, wearing Big Curly's boots, tromped over and kicked Sandy in the side. Mowrey started to protest, but the look in the Indian's eye kept her quiet.

A dazed and weakened Sandy Thompson couldn't fall asleep. The moon stood high over the trees. The pain of his arm nagged at every thought until his head pounded against the dirt and rocks he was lying on. Although he was pointed in the opposite direction of the fire, he could see the shadow of an Indian guard watching him throughout the night. Sandy kept hoping he could fall asleep. He tried to imagine happier times. He tried to plot another escape attempt. He even tried praying, something that he hadn't spent much time doing in the past few years.

Finally, he dozed off and dreamed of shallow graves. When he awoke, he ached all over. Dew soaked his clothes. The hard ground caused every joint to throb. His wrists and ankles were raw from the binding pressure of the rawhide ties and his sliced arm felt like fire. He tried to roll over on his back to get a better view.

The Bannocks had broken camp. As his eyes brought things into focus he could see they were all mounted, ready to head out. His condition must have looked obvious. They hadn't bothered tying him to a tree.

Mowrey was on Sandy's horse. One of the braves held the reins. "You've got to leave him something," she called out to Spotted Horse.

"I don't have to even leave him his scalp, Nez Percé!"

She pointed to the flour sack from Polly's in Ogden that was tied to the back of his saddle. "Let me throw down his grub bag at least. He'll never make it up that hill without food." She made a wide waving motion to a rocky hill toward the south.

"Give him the sack, woman, and get going." Spotted Horse commanded the brave with the reins, "Keep her quiet. I don't want to hear her voice again until we get to Fort Hall."

Sandy agonized for a half hour, trying to undo the food sack. He smiled on seeing the Confederate pistol and ammo tucked in with the apples and beans and jerky. The tight leather straps around his wrists and ankles started to loosen a little as the summer sun warmed the little clearing in which he lay. It was noon before he was able by brute force to stretch the leather and pull himself free from his bonds. He was hurt too much to walk or even stand.

He did manage to chew on some jerky. By then he was dying of thirst, and after a short rest he hobbled over to the creek to soak his hands, get a drink, and plump up some of the dried apples.

He analyzed his situation. He had food, a gun, and enough bullets to shoot some game. He was sore, wounded, and on foot. Behind was Ogden. He might be considered a horse thief or worse there. Had he been cleared from the shooting? Had Patty found his gold watch? He could not be sure. Besides, Ogden could prove to be a hot, dry, windy walk.

He could follow the Bannocks, but he'd never catch them by foot, and he had no idea how to capture a whole band of Indians. Somewhere to the north waited Montana Mudd. He detested the man more every minute.

Sandy retied the bandage on his arm and ate an apple. His numb fingers began to regain feeling. Mowrey's last words kept going over in his mind. She had thrown down the grub bag because she said he'd need strength for climbing the mountain. But the granite hill seemed the most unlikely direction to go. It was the kind of mountain that no one would climb unless he had to. He wondered why she had made such a big point of it. After washing off his face again with the cold creek water, he decided to investigate the mountain.

He threw the sack over his shoulder, tucked the .36 in his holster, and pressed uphill. Halfway up, his lungs ached and his arm throbbed so much he flopped down to catch his breath. He was able to look out across the tops of surrounding trees, but he saw no sign of any movement.

A look at the wound revealed that it was a clean cut, with not much swelling or pus. But it still bled a little. He rewrapped the bandage and pushed on uphill. When he finally dragged himself to the top, he found a welcome sight. A stubby pine with lightning-burned top held No-Neck's big roan, tied to a lower branch. He was saddled and waiting.

Sandy loosened the cinch and rubbed the horse's nose. Then he led it over the side of the mountain and the two of them slid their way to the bottom.

The pieces started fitting together. The single tracks yesterday up the mountain's backside belonged to Mowrey. For some reason she had gone straight up the mountain instead of following the Indian tracks as Sandy had. Then she had found the horse, left him tied, and somehow ended up captured by the Indians.

He pulled the saddle off the horse and led him over to the creek. He let him eat a little grass before refitting him for a long ride. With a horse, the situation changed. There was no doubt where Sandy would go. He would try to rescue Mowrey. It was the right thing to do. *Code of the West, and all that,* Sandy thought. *Or maybe it's in the Bible somewhere.*

While he resaddled No-Neck's horse, he tried to think of a plan of attack.

He knew he couldn't sneak up on the Indians very well. They had about five hundred years of trail smarts head start on him. But he was going to keep his pledge to No-Neck, or die trying. Sandy figured he had three things going for him. First, the Indians were weighed down with all the pack animals, so they couldn't move too fast. Second, they didn't expect him to follow, so there could be a surprise element if he was careful . . . and lucky. Third, he figured that Mowrey would surely do her best to slow the Indians down even more, since she could guess his movements once he found the horse.

He mounted up and rode until dark. By all rights he should have been getting weaker and weaker. But just the opposite was happening. It had always been that way. Put him on horseback, send him out through the wilderness, and something about wind in the face, the rhythm of the ride, and the solitude gave him new strength.

He pulled the saddle off the horse and pegged him down in a little meadow. Sandy found a spot back among the cottonwoods. He didn't build a fire, since he was unsure just where the Indians might be. He chewed on the jerky and apples and watched the stars come out. He thought about staying awake, just in case there was trouble, but he slept soundly.

By daybreak he was pushing the old roan up a nearby mountain to survey the area. A broad, open prairie stretched ahead in the far horizon. He knew he had to plan his attack before they all reached the flatland. There was no hope of surprise out there. From where he sat in the saddle, he thought he could see a puff of smoke swirling far to the north end of the valley. He considered the unpleasant thought of catching up to them by way of the switchback trail along the creek. It looked very narrow, long, and obvious. It wandered through several more little valleys before emptying out into the flatlands.

Sandy gambled that the trail the Bannocks traveled followed that creek all the way to the prairie. If he could make it up and over a couple of mountain ridges, perhaps he could intercept the party before they reached the open range. That meant a torturous ride right over the top of a couple of granite-covered ridges. If he made it, perhaps he could arrange an ambush. If not . . . at this point Sandy refused to speculate.

No-Neck's horse happened to be one in a hundred. "Any horse that could climb up that shale mountain," he said to the horse as they rode, "surely can cross these granite slopes." What the horse lacked in speed, he made up with surefootedness. A bit past noon they came down the last of the mountain ridges and caught back up with the trail. The lack of fresh tracks encouraged Sandy.

Their rough journey over loose rocks, steep slopes, and fallen logs may have been worth it. As long as this was the right trail, he had a chance at rescuing Mowrey and the hides.

Sandy examined his surroundings with care. It was a hot summer day, and this close to the prairie the grass along the trail was dried brown. The trail followed the creek that twisted its way out into the flatlands. The east side of the trail housed the ridge of mountains that Sandy just descended. Immediately to the west of the trail was the creek that had gained some volume as it made its way out of the mountains.

For most of the way the trail was up on a ledge, high above where the spring flood waters crashed along the creek earlier in the year. But just to the left Sandy spotted where the trail was forced down on the embankment and right along the creek itself. Granite boulder rockslides narrowed the passageway.

Sandy grabbed a long piece of deadwood at the creek's edge and climbed up on the bank at one of the narrowest spots. By wedging the wood behind some exposed granite boulders he caused an avalanche that blocked the trail. It wasn't even a very good barrier, but he counted on the possibility that even trail-wise Indians might be caught off guard.

He swept out his own tracks with a pine branch and staked the roan far out of sight. With a loaded .36, pockets crammed with ammunition, and a hunk of jerky to chew, he waited for the unsuspecting band.

For over two hours he saw no living thing. Not an Indian, not a deer, not a marmot, not a hawk, nothing. He had secured himself behind some of the downed boulders. It was good cover, but it meant sitting in the glaring sunlight. Still, he didn't dare to move. This time they would walk into his ambush.

There could always be another trail out into the prairie, he thought. He was about ready to abandon the idea and backtrack, when the band suddenly appeared.

Sandy sized up his adversary. There were three Indians at the lead, and one of them was Spotted Horse. No-Neck's string of horses followed. A brave led Mowrey. The others straggled behind. *Too many to fight,* Sandy concluded. *Somehow I've got to get at Spotted Horse, one to one.*

He saw his opportunity. Spotted Horse dismounted and attempted to clear the trail. As he struggled with a large stone, Sandy jumped him. The Confederate .36 was jammed into the muscular Indian's ear.

"I should have killed you, yellow hair. Reservation life has made me too soft."

"We all make mistakes." Sandy made sure the Indian could see the hammer cocked on the pistol. The others approached suddenly with rifles raised. Spotted Horse's body shielded Sandy.

"It's your move, yellow hair," the Bannock leader chided.

"I want the girl and my horse and the whole pack. Then, I want all of your guns to the ground and you Indians about a hundred miles out there on the prairie."

"You are still very stupid, yellow hair. Let me tell you what is going to happen. Your only chance is to make a run for your horse. Maybe my braves will miss you, but I doubt it. You're a dead man, yellow hair."

Then he twisted slightly toward the others. "If he tries anything, shoot the girl."

Two rifles closed in on Mowrey. "You harm that girl and the chief here is a dead man."

"Shoot the girl!" Spotted Horse barked the command.

Sandy screamed a warning. "You're killing your own leader if you do."

The braves sat with rifles raised and pointed at Mowrey.

"Yellow hair, you shoot me and you'll have no chance of escape. You'll be dead before I hit the ground. Shoot the Nez Percé!"

Sandy heard the cocking of a carbine.

"Wait a minute!" Sandy could feel the strain on his weak arm. "Look, there's no reason for anyone to be killed. You can have the pack, the hides, the whole works. Leave me the girl and the horse she rides on and the chief. As soon as you're on your way to the flatlands, I'll let the boss man here go. He can walk out to meet you. You can go home to Fort Hall, and we'll head back up into the mountains."

One of the Indians lifted his rifle toward Mowrey's head.

"Wait!" Spotted Horse showed his first sign of negotiation. "There might be a deal here." Sandy noticed Mowrey visibly relax. "But this is your last chance, white man. You can have the girl and her horse. That's all. We ride down the trail to the prairie with the rest, and I lead the way."

"You expect me to turn you loose? Now you're the crazy one."

"Shoot the girl!" Spotted Horse ordered once more.

"Wait!" This time Mowrey spoke. "Do what he says, Thompson. We don't need those hides."

Sandy knew that time was not on his side. Any second now one of those braves could get a clear shot at him.

"You saying I should trust an Indian?" he looked at her.

"I'm saying you should trust two Indians— Spotted Horse and me."

"Crazy woman," one of the braves sneered. "He doesn't care about you, he wants those hides just like we do."

Sandy knew he must move quickly now. "Release the girl. When she rides up the trail out of sight, then I'll let the chief go."

"Let her go!" Spotted Horse yelled.

Mowrey didn't hesitate to ride hard to the north and over the draw at a turn in the trail. Sandy freed the Indian, but kept the pistol cocked and aimed at his head.

"You made a good choice, yellow hair." The chief mounted and led the group to wade out into the creek and around the boulders. Sandy still expected them to turn on him. Spotted Horse looked back at Sandy and smiled.

"How do you know I won't come after those hides?" Sandy ventured.

"Because you are too smart to try to catch us on the prairie."

"How do I know you won't follow me back into the mountains to get the girl?"

"If we wanted the girl, we'd shoot you right now. You can have her. She'd make a bad wife. 'Do this, do that.' She's soured. Too much white man's blood. She's your fight now."

Then Spotted Horse turned and led the Indians out into the prairie. Sandy kept his gun aimed. He could have shot the chief at any time. When the last of the group edged over the horizon of the trail, he got his horse and rode to find Mowrey. She waited in the shade of the trees.

"How did you know they would leave without a fight?" he asked.

"I prayed about it. God hears Indians, too, you know."

"Yeah, well, I don't think they were going to shoot you back there. I mean, all they wanted was the hides."

"That's probably true. And they certainly don't like dying any more than we do. But I believe they would have shot me. You see, you didn't give the chief any other choice. If he didn't lead his braves out into the prairie, he would have lost his leadership. For him there would be no reason to go on living. Either he led them out, or he died trying. He was serious. By the way, what took you so long?"

"What took me so long? If you'll remember, I was bound, bleeding, and on foot."

"I left you a horse."

"Yeah, well, thanks. Anyway, I got you out. Do you think we should follow them?"

"Not on your life. We wouldn't have a chance out on the flatland."

"Will they follow us?"

Mowrey laughed. "For hides? Yes. For a Nez Percé woman? No way."

"The chief said you were a fighter. What did he mean? Are you all right? Did they mistreat you?"

Mowrey dropped her head. Sandy thought he detected a slight quiver on her lips. "Listen, if they laid a hand on you I'll go back out there and kill every one of those. . . ."

Mowrey spoke, but Sandy couldn't hear her muffled voice. "What did you say?"

She sat up straight. "I said, 'They treated me bad, they did not give me any dried apples.'"

"But what I meant was. . . ."

"I know what you meant, Thompson. But I think that if anybody has dried apples and doesn't share them, that is mistreating, don't you?" Mowrey flashed a sassy grin.

Sandy sighed, dug into his grub bag, and handed the girl a dried apple. "Mowrey, be serious. What I'm trying to find out is . . . well. . . ."

"No, Thompson, they didn't touch me. Why are you so interested in that?"

Sandy didn't answer. He just rode on.

"Where are we going?" she finally asked.

"First, we need to go to Mud Flats. Can you get us there?"

"Sure."

"Then we'll aim for Three Forks."

"I'm not going back there."

"Yes, you are. I made your father a promise, and I say you are going back."

"And I say that will never happen!" She kicked her horse and galloped up the trail ahead of Sandy.

CHAPTER
6

The hot sun burned their foreheads for over three hours before either of them spoke again. It was Mowrey who cleared her throat and turned to the man from Virginia whom she'd known for just a few days. "Thompson. . . ." She hesitated, waiting for the slim man with the hardened eyes to bolt his daydreams and join hers.

Sandy's mind had not been idle. He was scanning the trail ahead, pausing to look behind, staring for signs along the mountainside. In addition, his thoughts jumped from Mowrey to Mudd to the army sergeant, who reminded him of someone he'd like to forget, to the gunman that he let slip away because he was tired of killing. His army instinct warned him he'd regret that choice.

"Thompson!" The voice was more persistent now. Sandy pivoted to Mowrey's direction. She turned in her saddle in such a way as to complement her figure.

Suddenly he blurted out, "Hey, do you have another dress besides that one?"

"What?"

"You wear that buckskin all the time. I just wondered if you had some other dress. You know, gingham or calico?"

"Why should I have more than one dress? I only have one body," she shot back. "Why did you ask such a question?"

"Never mind, forget it. What was it you wanted?"

"Have I ever lied to you, Thompson?"

"Lied? How do I know if you've lied?"

"Just answer yes or no. Have I ever lied?"

"So you haven't lied. What has that to do with anything?"

"Because I'm not lying to you now. I'm not going back to that white woman's boarding school. It's not a good place to stay. I want you to take me back to my people."

"Your people, huh? Now, just where is that?" Sandy stopped the horses near a small creek, loosed their cinches, and dug into his bag for something to eat.

"I've got folks in Oregon, up in the Wallowas. But I'd settle for Lapwai in a pinch." Her voice was determined, serious.

"Look, I'm sorry you're separated from your tribe, and I'm sorry about your parents. But I promised No-Neck, so I have no choice."

"Why? Why do you have to keep a promise made to the dead? I'm alive, and I'm telling you I'm too old and too. . . ." She stopped.

"Too what?" he pushed his brown hat back and wiped his brow.

"Well, the Indian word is . . . too ripe. You won't believe what goes on up there."

"Like it or not, I'm taking you back. I know that No-Neck will never know if I kept my promise. But I would. I would know that my word isn't good. I would know that I'm not to be trusted. And when you live like that, it's a fearful thing. Rain or shine, kick or scream, I'm taking you there. What you do after that is your own business."

They mounted up and rode the trail again.

"Thompson, have you ever been to one of these buffalo hunters' rendezvous?"

"No, what can I expect?"

"Well, my father says it is not like the old days. I mean, the big days of trapping ended over thirty years ago. Back then, they say there were beaver holed up on every creek. They caught them by the thousands. It's all changed. Buffalo's the only thing that's plentiful. Unless you know a few secret places like my father. The rendezvous at Henry's Fork is mainly an excuse for men to talk about the good old days and sell their hides. No-Neck was one of the last who actually made money trapping. This year's reunion is mainly a wild time for some gray-haired men and their dreams."

They climbed a moderately steep granite incline. The evening sky glowed a bright orange as they settled down in camp for the night. The food now depleted, Mowrey built a fire anyway.

"If I had a pole, I'd pull one of those juicy trout out of the creek," Sandy offered.

"We'll have trout," Mowrey replied matter-of-factly.

"What are you going to do, catch one with your hands?" Sandy retorted. He chafed at Mowrey's continual confidence.

Mowrey pulled off her moccasins at the water's edge. She lifted her buckskin skirt knee-high and waded slowly into the frigid waters of Broken Bow Creek. She leaned against the force of the current in the middle of the stream, just above a small pool of isolated calm in the swirl of the white water. She stood, stooped at the waist, holding her buckskin in one hand, hovered above the water like an osprey ready to dive. Suddenly, she jerked her hand into the pool and yanked out a slippery, kicking trout.

Sandy stared with his mouth open. "How did you do that?" he shouted above the noise of the creek. She motioned for him to be silent and waded over to hand him the fighting fish. Then she returned to the middle of the creek. This time she crouched at a different spot. For a long time she made no movement at all. Then once again, she hauled out a huge fish and headed for shore.

Sandy was sure that the broiled trout was the finest fish dinner he had ever eaten.

It hadn't broken daylight when he roused out of his bedroll and built a fire. He looked over at Mowrey. She always slept the same. Flat on her back, blanket pulled over her face and wrapped around her head. Only her two closed eyelids could be seen. *It must be nice to be so short that a six-foot blanket will wrap around your head,* he thought. Tall Sandy Thompson had never found a blanket long enough to cover him.

He warmed up and then wandered along the creek in search of game. As he stared at the creek in the early morning dawn, he thought about wading into the water and trying his hand at fish catching. Wisdom, and a small antelope buck, convinced him otherwise.

It would take a good shot to bring down the little fellow, and the Bannocks had his Winchester. All he possessed was his Rigdon and Ansley .36 pistol. The animal froze and tilted its ears in Sandy's direction. One hundred feet away the .36 carefully charted the antelope's moves. The buck lapped the clear creek water once more. It was his last.

The revolver shattered the peaceful morning air. The animal bolted toward the woods with the .36 bullet lodged deep in its throat. It only made two steps when a second bullet caught it just behind the ear.

"Good shooting," Mowrey hollered down from a red sandstone bluff behind him. "I mean, for a greenhorn with a pistol."

Sandy held his tongue. He didn't feel like getting into another verbal volley with Mowrey. He looked forward to transporting her to the Indian school.

By the third day they rode close to the rendezvous, up the Henry's Fork, through Bear Gulch, and onto the flats. Steep granite walls guarded the east and west sides. A narrow trail led north. Only the south afforded a broad clearance. Mowrey and Sandy entered there. Assorted columns of smoke drifted through the tall pines of the valley floor. There were tents, stock, and log cabins scattered around with a semblance of a pattern. Along the west wall a band of Indians camped. *Mowrey was right,* Sandy thought. *It had seen its better days.* A bunch of tired-looking old men remained.

He followed Mowrey through the camps to a clearing at the north end of the canyon. A dozen men lined up, aiming their rifles at a man about one hundred yards away. Except for the distance between them, it looked like a firing squad. Sandy squinted his eyes for a closer look at the condemned man. "It's Mudd!" he shouted.

He spurred his horse toward the riflemen. "Don't shoot him until I get my money!" he yelled. He fired a warning shot in the air. The men turned and stared as he rode up and jumped to the ground. "No doubt Mudd deserves what you're about to do," he began, "but let me talk to him first. He's got my money."

"Shoot him?" drawled a heavy Texan. "We ain't

gonna shoot him. We was just finishin' one of his contests."

"Contest?" Sandy repeated as he pushed his hat back.

"Sure." The spokesman pulled out a wad of tobacco and offered some to Sandy. He declined. "We all gave Mudd a dollar. Then we shoot those old peach cans he tosses up. If you miss one, you're out. Last one in wins a keg of Mudd's best whiskey."

Mudd, who was too far away to know what was going on, hollered for the next contestant to get ready.

"Can I get in on this?" Sandy asked.

"Don't know. Who are you, anyway?" The Texan looked down the row at the others. "Don't believe we've seen you at the rendezvous before."

"I'm Sandy Thompson. I traveled with No-Neck Mowrey when he fell at the hands of some bush-whackers."

"They got No-Neck?"

"Buried him next to Mink Creek, back in the Wasatch. Bannocks took his string. I'm taking his daughter to a school in Montana. Meantime, Mudd knows about some stolen money of mine. Now, can I borrow your gun for the contest?"

"Here, Thompson, use mine." A wiry man handed him a Winchester. "I'm gonna tell the others about No-Neck." He scurried away.

Mudd started tossing cans. Shots rang from one

wall of the canyon to the other. One by one the marksmen were eliminated. Finally, three remained—Sandy; the Texan, Wayne Jared; and a muzzle-loader. The muzzle-loader shot first. He blasted the can fifty feet north of Mudd. Then the Texan took another chaw of tobacco, spit, and fired. He missed.

Sandy's shot found a target. He and the old man went two more rounds. Then the old man missed. "Barrel's too hot," he explained. "Can't shoot this old pilgrim that often. Too bad, too. I could already taste that rattlesnake juice of Mudd's burning through my gut."

"Stick around, old-timer," Sandy advised. "I haven't shot yet."

"You ain't likely to miss with that Winchester."

"Well, what you don't know is I don't like strychnine squeezings, and I have a little something extra planned for the final shot. Just watch."

Mudd threw the can high as usual. This time Sandy aimed elsewhere. About the time the can should have been blasted, Mudd's dirty black hat flew off his head. "Shucks." Sandy grinned. "I missed. I guess we tied, and you can have my half," he told the old man.

By now Mudd was screaming and running as fast as his round body could move. "Which one of you drunken, half-breed jackasses—" Then he spotted Sandy. "Why . . . why, partner, it's you.

What took you so long? I figured you'd be here long ago."

Sandy kept his rifle pointed at Mudd. "I want to see my money."

Montana Mudd looked puzzled. "Money? I remember promising to outfit you in good fashion, but I don't recall owing you any money. . . ." His words were cut off by the hammer being pulled back on Sandy's rifle. The others around them backed away.

"Mudd, listen up. If you don't return my money, chances are these will be the last words you hear short of the pearly gates. I got off the train in Ogden, got stuck eating with you at Patty's. Then you got me mixed up with some gunslingers. Before I could bow out, I was struck in the head and left for dead. There wasn't anyone in that whole outfit that knew I was carrying gold coins except you. And you conveniently disappeared. Now, I figure you're down to your last few minutes of breath, so don't fritter them away with hogwash. Where's my money?"

Sandy didn't know if he was bluffing or not. It was not his custom to do his reasoning from behind the trigger. He grew up believing men were rational animals. But experience has a way of destroying fantasies. The war, the running west, the past few weeks made his gun quicker than the tidier forms of justice. But when push came to shove, Sandy doubted if he would pull the trigger.

Mudd must have figured the same thing. Either that, or he was too dumb to be scared. He took out a chaw and spit in the general direction of a small spruce. "Now, son," he said calmly, "I'm sure sorry for any trouble I caused you. But I see the story different. I did befriend you to get some of your money. But I wanted it fair and square. I thought I could talk you into buying some of my supplies. As far as the incident down at Patty's, I was merely trying to save my skin. Those boys meant business. Even though I didn't owe them a dollar, they weren't in reasonable moods. When I hit the livery and caught my horse, I figured they'd follow me and leave you alone, I had no idea you'd get slapped down. Tell you what—you take any of those fellas for a witness. You can search through all my belongings. If you find your money, I'll give it back and give you an outfit besides. Don't know what else to do. Does that sound fair, boys?" He played to the trapper and trader jury that knew him best. Sandy assumed it wouldn't take much to turn the whole camp against an outsider like himself.

Sandy lowered the rifle, and spoke in the slow Southern drawl that forever identified him with a war that was lost. "Mudd, I'll go you one further. I'll search your stuff, all right. If I don't find the gold coins, then we'll split your entire stock right down the middle—fifty-fifty."

"What?" Mudd sputtered like he'd just swallowed his chew. "You'll what?"

"Look, Mudd, I got into this mess because you falsely, and knowingly, called me your partner. If you can't pay me back my money, then we really are partners. I want my share."

It didn't take long to sort through Mudd's supplies and gear. There was no sign of the missing money. "Well, Mudd, that makes us partners. I'll be taking my half now!"

"Wait!" Mudd complained. "You can't do that!"

Sandy appealed to the hangers-on for support. "What did Mudd call me the minute he recognized who I was?"

"Why, he called you 'partner,'" one of them replied. The others mumbled agreement.

Mudd searched for a way out. "But . . . but . . . that won't hold. That's just a term of affection to a friend, you know."

Sandy began his own appeal for justice. "Now, men, would you say that this gold-toothed, foul-smelling, cheap-whiskey trader and I have much affection for each other?"

Wayne Jared guffawed. "Not hardly. You act more like partners than friends, if you ask me."

Clarence Earl Mudd wasn't about to stand idly by and watch half his worldly riches disappear. Instead, he chose to do something no decent trader ever dreamed of. He stormed off to drink some of his own whiskey.

The muzzle-loader introduced himself. "The name's Pop Bradley." He helped Sandy divvy up Mudd's supplies. Sandy's share: 126 buffalo hides, fair condition; 36 assorted beaver and small animal hides; 2 pack mules; an Appaloosa mare; a small keg of flour; a keg of beans; a keg of nails. Thrown into the pile was some rock salt, molasses, several cans of fruit and tomatoes, a big string of dried apples, 2 bolts of cloth, and 2 slightly worn, but handsome, Winchester rifles.

Sandy made sure he had enough ammunition to keep the rifles smoking. In addition, he acquired some shovels, picks, and pans, just in case some gold cried out to be panned.

Pop settled into drinking the better part of the keg he'd won in the shooting contest. Sandy knew he didn't want all that stuff, so he decided to stick around and try to trade some of it. As he headed down to the next camp he observed the Indian teepees again. For the first time in hours he remembered Mowrey. He made his way over to the Indian encampment in hopes that Mowrey had gone there.

The evening cook fires began to blaze, and some of the Indians gathered around a game with rocks and small holes dug into the ground. "Have you seen an Indian girl in a buckskin dress?" The minute the words came out Sandy realized how foolish that sounded. "I mean, one called Mowrey?"

"Are you the yellow hair that brought her here?" A brawny brave looked up from the game. He repeated the words in Crow to the others. Immediately, Sandy found himself surrounded by a dozen knives and guns.

It was time for fast talking. "Look, we came in together because I promised her father I'd take her to Montana."

The brave challenged Thompson. "The Nez Percé girl says that you were a friend of her father's, but that you don't like her very much. She fears harm."

"Don't like her? Of course I like her. Just tell me where she is and I won't bother you anymore." Sandy began to push through the crowd.

"You like her?" the brave pressed.

"I said I like her. We're friends. She's just upset about losing her father and all."

The young warrior threw out a further challenge. "Well, let me tell you something, yellow hair. I like her, too."

"Hey, now let's get this thing right," Sandy said with his hand on his gun.

"If you're planning to ride out of here with her," the brave continued, "you'll have to fight me first."

"I can't believe this. Where's Mowrey? Let me talk to her."

"Will you fight?" the brave dared. "Or is your back the same color as your hair?"

The words hadn't cleared the man's lips before Sandy's right hand smashed into the jawbone of the Crow warrior. At the same time, his gun was out and cocked, aimed at the eldest man in the circle. "Now, listen real careful—at least two, maybe three of you are going to die before you can finish me, so why don't you let me know who wants the first bullet?" After a moment of silence, he added, "Now, as I asked before, where's Mowrey?"

"So, you will fight for her." The brave rose while rubbing his jaw. "I will see you at dawn in the meadow. At dawn, yellow hair."

Sandy backed out of the camp with caution. Just as he cleared the edge of the encampment, a young Indian girl motioned to him from behind a tall sage. She pointed to Sandy, outlined a woman's shape with her hands, pointed to herself, then down a trail.

"What do you want?" Sandy demanded.

The girl grew excited, impatient. She held her nose from underneath with her index finger and thumb. Then, she motioned Sandy to hurry.

Watching the girl hold her nose made him blurt out, "Mudd! Did that stinking, filthy Mudd send you here? You tell him—"

"No!" she protested, then once again held her nose.

"Nose held . . . circle nose, ring nose, pierced nose . . . Nez Percé! You want to take me to a Nez Percé? To Mowrey?"

She nodded. They rushed along the bluff to the back side of another group of tents. They approached one tent and the girl motioned Sandy to sit down close to the back of the tent. The girl then entered the tent from the front. Soon Sandy heard Mowrey's voice.

"Thompson, is that you?"

"Of course it's me. What's going on here? Get your horse and let's pack up. I've got some supplies. We can go right now."

"I can't. You see, when we came here I was convinced you wouldn't take me to my people. So I looked for another way. I thought these Crow were going north. When I asked to travel along until they came to the Nez Percé, they agreed. But now I learn that Little Wolf intends for me to be his bride. And they're going back to Yellowstone. Thompson, I don't want to be a Crow squaw! They're proud, strong people. Sometimes the warriors are vicious and cruel, not only with their enemies, but with their wives as well. But I will have to stay unless you win the fight tomorrow."

"Fight? You don't think I'm going to fight for you, do you?"

"Certainly!" she said in her assured manner. "I remember a man who had to keep a promise to a friend. Something about not being able to live with himself. Well, allowing the Crow to capture me and force me to marry one of them isn't keeping your word to my father."

"Turning yourself in like this isn't exactly what I'd call 'being captured.' And this morning you weren't all that concerned about my keeping my word."

"That was this morning. Besides, you convinced me. It's a thing you call honor, I believe," came the reply from inside the tent.

"Look, Mowrey, I'm going to cut a hole in this tent. You get your things. Forget the horse. I've got another. We'll go now!"

"Don't do that!" she pleaded. "They won't let you!"

Sandy looked all around. He spied several Indians with rifles on the adjoining cliffs. They'd been watching the whole time. "They don't mind if we talk?" he queried with his eyes riveted on the guards.

"No, it's the custom. Both the prospective husbands have equal opportunity to talk to the bride, but they can't see her until after the fight."

"Husbands!" Sandy yelled. "Mowrey, I'm not your prospective husband. If I fight, it's for one reason only—to get you to that school in Three Forks. Are you going or not?"

There was a long pause inside. Finally she said faintly, "Yes, I will go."

Sandy hurried back toward the trappers. He needed to find out two things. First, where could he trade off some of his unwanted goods? Second, what would be expected of him in this duel at dawn?

He found Pop Bradley asleep on top of his buffalo hides, muzzle-loader in hand. He left him there to look for a trader. A Frenchman gave him a pound of gold nuggets for the hides and furs.

It was harder to get rid of the nails. They were so heavy that even though they were a valuable commodity, many travelers shied from carrying them. Finally, Sandy made a deal with a bearded trapper headed to Mormon country. He gave Sandy two buck knives, a flour sack full of dried elk, and a nearly new blue gingham dress. After the exchange, Sandy rested at the bonfire with at least two dozen other men.

"Hey," one of them called out, "ain't you Mudd's partner, the one who was with No-Neck when he went down?"

In the dark Sandy wasn't sure who had spoken, so he addressed the whole group. "Mudd and I have gone our separate ways. But, yes, I was there when they ambushed No-Neck. They hid out in the trees and opened fire as we rode in. No-Neck took a bad one first thing. But he kept fighting to the end."

"It would take more than a single gun to bring down No-Neck Mowrey." This time Sandy noticed a tall, slim man with a big wide hat.

"There were four. We got three of them. One threw down his gun and ran away."

"What did he look like? What kind of gun?"

Sandy wondered at the persistent curiosity. "The

man was about five-eleven, with long brown burnsides that sort of swung around to his mustache. His eyes were close together. He wore an old blue button-down bib shirt. I wouldn't miss him if I saw him again. But I reckon that's not likely."

"Don't bet on it," another man joined in. "What do you think, Branch, is that enough to go on?"

The man with the wide hat spoke. "That's enough for now. But it would be good if Thompson here would come with us. I'd hate to string up the wrong man. What do you say? You got the time?"

"Sorry, I've got to get to Montana, then to California. That man's probably in south Texas by now."

"That's what we figure too. Well, it ain't your battle, I guess," Branch said. "You see, there ain't no law in here yet. So we take care of things ourselves. If one of us goes down, the one who did it can figure to settle with at least a dozen others. It's what's supposed to keep every solo hunter and trapper from becoming easy prey to worthless drifters."

Sandy continued, "The man you want headed west from the upper meadows on Mink Creek. If you find him, I guarantee I'll be a witness against him . . . if you bring him in alive."

Sandy paused, then said as casually as possible, "By the way, just wondering, I've heard about these Indians fighting each other over who gets a certain squaw. What all's involved in a fight like that?"

The men picked right up on it. "Yeee-hah!"

"We got ourselves a fight coming on."

"We're rootin' for you, son."

"I suppose it's at sunrise."

"Who're you fighting?"

Sandy sighed. "Some brave named Little Wolf. But it's not what you think. No-Neck's daughter's in a jam, and fighting Little Wolf seems to be the only way out. Anyway, what can I expect?"

Wayne Jared filled him in. "If you're fighting Little Wolf, you can expect to get your head caved in, or a knife in your ribs, minimum. He's a mean one, strong as a wounded buffalo. What you did was get yourself in a fight to the finish. Now, mind you, you can always back out. But those Indians don't ever give up. They'd rather die than admit defeat. Personally, I don't know as a squaw's worth that much. But that's up to the man, now, ain't it?"

Another man piped in, "You ought to ask me. I sure know. Lost my arm to a cutthroat Black-foot. . . ." The man pointed to his empty sleeve.

Sandy pumped them. "So the two of us just show up in the morning and go to it fist and foot, teeth and toenail, until one of us quits kicking?"

The one-armed man commented, "That's about it. There'll be a couple hundred braves standing around rooting for Little Wolf, and, of course, we'll be there to root you on. Oh, yeah, and there'll be the shawnessos."

"The what?" Sandy wasn't sure he heard the man.

"A shawnesso's a kind of stand-in. He's someone who's allowed to help you out if you need to bandage a wound or catch your breath. The only problem is, you can use the shawnesso only once. After that, he can't enter the conflict. You bein' a stranger, I suppose you don't have one?"

Sandy ignored the question. "You mentioned knives. What's legal?"

"Besides knives, there's spears, rocks . . . it don't matter, just so both men have equal access to the same type weapon. If you don't carry a big knife, for instance, one of the braves will toss you one."

Sandy was deep in thought as the one-armed man deftly pulled out a pouch of tobacco and paper and rolled a cigarette with his one good hand. Meanwhile, another man joined the group, a dark-complected man with a black beaver top hat. He grabbed a cup of coffee and pulled back into the flickering shadows.

Suddenly Sandy slapped his knee and roared. As the others jumped, Sandy explained. "I've been fighting for ten years now. Started with the war. Now I come west and I fight river gamblers, Mexican federales, even a deranged bear. In the past two weeks alone I've been alley-belted, ambushed by murderous backsiders and Bannock Indians. Now I've got to fight a buck. It would be downright funny if it were happening to anyone else besides me. Fighting must be terminal once you start, like a disease. Makes a man not want to get up in the morning. I just keep thinking, what's next?"

"If your name's Thompson, I can tell you what's next." It was the newcomer in the beaver top hat.

Sandy peered through the shadows at the stranger. "Who are you?"

The man pushed the hat to the back of his head. He held the tin cup close to his lips and blew on the hot liquid. Finally he spoke. "I just rode in from Ogden. About a week ago had supper at a place down on Twenty-fifth Street. Patty's something or other. It was a Saturday night. The place was packed, so I joined a couple of fellas at a table. Turns out one of them's an army investigator. Anyway, he had on an army uniform and all, some stripes on the sleeve. The other man was about my size, bushy hair running around to his mouth. The thing I noticed was an engraved leather holster, but no pistol. No sir, just an empty pocket.

"I was sitting there eating my meat—now, you fellas really ought to try Patty's chili steak—and these two were making plans. They're teamed up to find a Virginian named Thompson. Something about a robbery back in the Shenandoah. So I figure if that's you, tomorrow's trouble should be sufficient for tomorrow. I think that's in the Good Book somewheres."

"Did you hear the army man's name?" Something in Sandy's gut told him he already knew the answer.

"The one with the empty holster was called T. The other . . . say, I didn't think I'd forget so soon. It was sort of funny, you know, a couple of words run together, like Goodman, or Greenough." The man paused to scratch his dusty forehead.

Sandy leaped to his feet. "Grandview! Was it Grandview?"

"That's it, sure enough. I see you know all about it." The man leaned over to grab the coffeepot that swung on an iron hook over a lower portion of the fire.

Sandy sat down, speechless.

A Scotsman named Ian carried on a conversation with the newcomer. "You say they wanted Thompson? The West is a mighty big place. It'll be hard to track him up here."

"I don't think so. They told Patty they were looking for an old friend. She said she thought you were headed to Mudd's place at Big Springs. I don't figure they'll be dumb enough to ride right into here, but mark my words, they'll be out there waiting."

All Sandy could think about was Grandview . . . and Fort John T. Edwards . . . and three gruesome months. Sandy was one of the lucky ones . . . he escaped.

Ian asked, "How come you're so sure they'll stick with it in this wild country? Must be something pretty big."

Branch interrupted. "This one called T.— sounds like our man, don't it, Thompson? You say the other one wore a uniform? Did it sound like official army business?"

"I ain't no expert," the stranger responded as he backed up closer to the fire. "But he looked like a renegade on his own to me."

"Fellas," Branch suddenly announced, "let's hit it. Thompson has enough to think about for one night."

One by one they slipped away to tents, wagons, bedrolls. A few stopped by to give Sandy some advice. But his mind wasn't on the upcoming fight. He gazed into the glowing coals while drawing an Arkansas whetstone across his sharp knife.

It was him on the train, Sandy realized. But no beard, no sword . . . and a sergeant now? Grandview was a captain before. But then, it had been a long time. Since July 14, 1867, to be exact. Corporal Theodore Thompson, C.S.A., was the first to testify against Captain Robert Grandview, officer in charge of Fort Edwards, prisoner of war camp. The authorities wanted to know why eighty-three Confederate soldiers died after the war had ended. Sandy knew why, and so did Grandview. Sandy told the court-martial judges the truth about Grandview. But, the verdict—demotion and hard labor—was strictly Yankee justice.

It's like the war . . . it just keeps right on following me, Sandy reflected.

The ground felt harder, the stars appeared more distant, the wind blew colder, and his mind flitted, more restless than ever. Sandy Thompson sensed he'd be turning some major corners soon.

"Lord," he mumbled, "life's got to be simpler than this. I'm tired of looking over my shoulder, tired of fighting someone else's fight, tired of never getting enough rest."

His words faded, yet he lay awake staring at the stars. Finally, he got up, pulled on his boots, and forced Grandview out of his mind. Right now he had the small matter of an Indian dispute.

CHAPTER
7

Armed with a bolt of cloth from Mudd's supplies, Sandy found a trapper with an extra pair of knee-high beaded moccasins to trade. Now he could shed his heavy boots and move quicker.

He laced up the moccasins with care, strapping his sheathed knife in the left one, ready for a right-handed cross-draw. He hoped he wouldn't have to use the knife. His strategy was simple—catch the Indian off guard early, then strike hard. That should end the whole thing in a hurry.

Pop Bradley and Wayne Jared stopped to talk. "What about a shawnesso?" they queried.

Sandy had forgotten about the stand-in. He really didn't plan to need one, or to give Little Wolf time to use his.

"Wayne and me been talkin'," Pop continued, "and we knowed that neither of us is worth much, but we'd both stand by you today, if you need help."

Sandy knew each of these men were crack shots with a rifle, but this wasn't a shooting contest. Besides, they had been drinking most the night. They'd be lucky to stay awake long enough to watch the fight, must less participate. He'd worry too much about them getting hurt. "Fellas, I appreciate the friendship, but I got to do this alone. Anyway, I've got a plan."

Wayne creased his forehead. "I hope you got two or three plans at least. Are you sure you know somethin' about fightin' Indians?"

"If I knew much about fighting Indians, I wouldn't be in this fix in the first place, now would I?" Sandy grinned for the first time that morning.

The scene developed just as the men had described the night before. A small meadow separated the Indian encampment from the trappers.

The grass had been grazed down to a nub. Even in the shadow of the Tetons it was baked hard as a dirt road. It wasn't quite daylight, but when Sandy arrived, several hundred Indians surrounded the meadow. An equal number of trappers and hunters faced them. It looked as though most of them had spent many hours drinking Mudd's whiskey, or worse.

Before Sandy entered the circle he found two round, fist-sized river rocks. He concealed them fairly well in his large bandana. Little Wolf waited for him as Sandy peeled off his plaid shirt. The closest spectators couldn't help but notice the scar. It ran from under his right arm and slanted around to the middle of his back. He also exposed the fairly new scar courtesy of the Bannocks. "Looks like you got caught in a mill saw," Pop called out.

"I've been in a scuffle or two," Sandy admitted. He surveyed the area before advancing closer to Little Wolf.

"Don't be hemmed in by the crowd," Bradley advised. "You've got the whole territory, not just the meadow. And don't count on that brave being predictable. They'll stand their ground when you think they should run. They'll jump when you think they're down. They'll holler when you expect quiet. Remember, he'll never give up. You'll have to knock him senseless or kill him. I suggest you kill him."

"Do you suppose you could find me two long army swords?" Sandy responded. "Hold them at the meadow's edge until I call out. I just might need them."

This wasn't a boxing match at Harvard, nor a river brawl on a steamboat. No preliminaries, no speeches, no rules, no one to sound a horn or declare a winner. On one side, a Crow Indian brave with breechcloth, painted face, and braided hair. On the other, a white man from Virginia, also in moccasins, his shiny blond hair reflecting the rising sun.

Little Wolf had slept little. This contest had taken on much more than amorous proportions for him. After all, Mowrey would just be another wife, and a talkative one at that. But for weeks Little Wolf had campaigned to convince his people that the time had come to drive the white man out of Crow land. The elders counseled against it. "They're too strong."

"We can't defeat them."

"We must learn to live with them."

Little Wolf despised such talk. He would show them how weak the white man really was. He would defeat the yellow hair swiftly, viciously. He could count on twenty-five braves to ride out with him once he proved his strength. Little Wolf hadn't once considered that he might lose. That is, until he detected the yellow hair's scar. An old superstition gripped him: "Man who fights close to death, then wants to fight again, is not afraid to die." For the first time he feared a long confrontation.

He crouched as Sandy approached. He barely saw the rock tossed high in his direction. "Catch, Little Wolf," Sandy yelled.

The Indian caught the rock. Then Sandy jumped, crashing down with the other rock on the Indian's head. That was Plan Number One. However, unpredictable elements intruded. Little Wolf cocked his head sideways to see the rock, so he wasn't blinded by the morning sun. Sandy's blow hit hard but glanced off. Before Sandy's blow fell, Little Wolf seized the rock out in front of him. At that same moment the brave struck hard into the Virginian's midsection.

Both contenders collapsed on the first blow. The crowd roared. As they struggled to stand, Sandy landed a couple of hard left-handed jabs to Little Wolf's jaw. On the third try, the Indian grabbed Sandy's arm, jerked him around, and sunk his teeth into the suntanned shoulder. Sandy yelped, then wildly flung his left elbow behind him, catching the Indian just above the left ear. Little Wolf fell. But before Sandy could check his wound, the Indian leapt high with knife in hand. Sandy backed off. The Indian shrieked a war cry and lunged forward.

Sandy tripped, then rolled as he hit the ground. He missed, by inches, the down-thrust blade of the buckhorn. Rising instantly to his feet, knife in hand, he faced Little Wolf. Breathing hard, each probed for an advantage, a first good blow to hold the upper hand. They circled cautiously. Suddenly, Little Wolf ran to the outside of the ring of shouting spectators. Sandy started to follow, then stopped. He remembered Pop Bradley's injunction about Indians doing the unexpected. He held his ground.

Little Wolf plowed around the perimeter once, then charged. Sandy braced himself for a leap, but the brave dove for his feet instead. The knife caught his left moccasin, slicing the buckskin from heel to knee. The shoe fell off, revealing a bloody gash. Sandy would have to continue barefoot and lame.

Survival began to overpower reason in Sandy's mind. This frightened him more than the brave. He knew survival gives strength, but reason gives advantage. He struggled while evading passes to develop an alternate strategy.

On a wild gamble, he turned and hurled his knife across the meadow. Honor dictated that Little Wolf pitch his knife, too. The Indian hesitated. His eyes glared. Ignoring the taunts of his friends, he threw his weapon to the ground.

Sandy immediately attacked. He plunged in with punches to the midriff. Little Wolf returned blow for blow. They could hardly keep standing. Sandy squatted, then raised his head up hard, crashing into the Indian's chin. Sandy heard Little Wolf's teeth and jawbone shatter. The Indian groaned on the ground. Sandy could stand, but his head whirled. He could barely hear the cries of the rooters, and only faintly did he hear the appeal, "Shawnesso!"

A blurred mountain advanced toward Sandy. As it drew closer, Sandy perceived an Indian form that moved like a bear, armed with a wide-blade bowie knife. Sandy couldn't move. He struggled for air enough in his aching lungs to mutter, "Shawnesso?"

"Here I am, partner!" A bloodcurdling scream resounded from behind him. Even the human bear stopped in his tracks. From fifty feet away Montana Mudd lumbered across the field, knife in hand. He was drunk, but he stormed straight toward the oncoming Indian shawnesso. The huge Indian braced for the battle. Mudd startled him by throwing the knife instead. The blade sank to the hilt into the left lung.

The Indian jerked the knife out and charged Mudd, a weapon in each hand. Two gallons of whiskey lost their effect. Mudd retreated, fast. A sober Clarence Earl Mudd scrambled back three steps, then gasped as the giant collapsed two feet in front of him.

Meanwhile, Sandy had recovered somewhat, just in time to encounter a hate-filled Little Wolf, battered jaw hanging to one side. Animal impulses had taken over. Sandy knew the time had come for Plan Number Two. He called to Pop for the long swords. Sandy tossed one to the brave. Little Wolf didn't reach for it. It was a white man's weapon, the weapon of a soldier.

Sandy seized the advantage. He appealed to the onlookers. "Come on, pick it up. Pick it up, Little Wolf. Or maybe its Little Mouse instead. Pick it up, Little Mouse." The trappers repeated the chant, "Little Mouse, Little Mouse. . . ." The Indians screamed, "No!"

Little Wolf snatched up the cold steel. He soon realized his mistake. The sword was Sandy's favorite sparring tool. He knocked the sword out of the Indian's hand and kicked him hard to the ground. Sandy held the long blade with both hands on the hilt above his downed opponent. Half the crowd jeered, "Scalp him! Scalp him!"

Sandy plunged the sword into the ground just inches from the barely conscious Indian's neck. He pressed his weight on the sword, then angled it so the sharp steel stuck an inch from Little Wolf's throat. He grabbed the other blade, and with his last ounce of strength, he shoved it into the earth. The weapons now crossed at the Indian's neck. If he tried to raise up, he'd slice his own throat. If he attempted to pull out the swords, he'd slice his hands. He did not move.

Sandy limped back to the cheering trappers and hunters. Pop met him with a large bandana for his leg. Wayne Jared poured whatever he was drinking on the shoulder bite. Sandy's cry of pain was drowned out by a piercing shriek from the meadow.

Little Wolf had recognized his dilemma. He had been defeated by a yellow hair. He'd lost his standing with the warriors because he hadn't fought until death. He had no future except as a fire-builder or water-carrier. With all the strength he could muster, he thrust himself into the blades, nearly decapitating himself.

The sight made Sandy turn his head. "You gave him no choice," Pop said matter-of-factly.

Sandy tried to walk away. A female voice called after him, "Thompson! Thompson!"

He glanced in the direction of the red bluff. "Thompson!" Mowrey yelled again as she ran toward him.

Those who watched weren't sure if it was the force of her body hurled against him as she jumped into his arms, or the words that she spoke that made him collapse.

"Now we'll be married!" she announced confidently.

Sandy dreamed he was in church in Virginia. His sister was singing a song about joy. She smiled and clapped her hands. He was delirious with happiness, and then. . . . He squinted his eyes up at some rough log rafters and tried to get his bear-

125

ings. It wasn't home. There was no brick wall or white painted woodwork. Besides, he remembered that his home burned down.

It wasn't the Louisiana swamps—no moss in the tree overhead. It wasn't Fort Edwards—no bars on the windows, no stench. Henry's Fork . . . trapper's rendezvous . . . Mud Flats . . . Ogden . . . Mudd . . . Mowrey . . . Mowrey!

Sandy leaned on his elbow to survey the place. A torn buffalo robe hung in the doorway of a small, dilapidated two-room cabin. Between the shreds of the robe he saw several men sitting around a table playing cards. There was Mudd, Pop Bradley, Wayne Jared, and the man known as Branch. Next to the fireplace, head in hands, sat Mowrey.

Sandy could tell it was daylight, only he didn't know which day. "I'm not getting married!" he bellowed with vehemence to those in the other room. A rush of motion followed.

Pop carried in a full coffee cup. Wayne peeled off the bandana from Sandy's injured foot. "Where am I?" Sandy murmured, quieter.

"Why, you're in Muddville, of course. I thought you'd know, partner!" Sandy couldn't mistake the voice.

"I thought we ended the partnership, Mudd . . . but I appreciate the hospitality. How long have I been lying here?"

Branch said, "Almost twenty-four hours, I'd say."

"You were a might tuckered out after that dance with Little Wolf," Pop continued. "We hauled you here to rest yesterday morning. You must be powerful hungry. Let me get you something—"

"I will get his food," Mowrey announced.

"Did you hear what I said, Mowrey?" Sandy insisted again.

She didn't answer as she scurried to warm up beans, meat, and bread.

Mowrey knew not to press the point. She had agreed to go to Three Forks without protest, and she would. However, she had decided that if she had to marry a white man, Thompson would do just fine.

Sandy hobbled into the front room to join the men at the table. They told him all the Indians had pulled out after the duel. Most of the trappers began to leave, too. The sight of Little Wolf lingered in all their minds. Fear of trouble from the Indians returned. Some talked about not meeting at Mud Flats anymore.

"Who are we kidding?" Branch said. "There's nothing left to trap anyway. Most of us gather here to get drunk. We might as well sell our hides in Bozeman. The prices are the same. Seems to me we just got one piece of unfinished business. Some guy named T. thinks he can ambush hunters and trappers and get away with it. Before I set another trap line, I'm going to make sure that one's hanging."

"How many you figure will go with us?" Pop inquired.

Branch rubbed his beard. "Well, I've got twenty-five or thirty who say they'll ride, but we'll be lucky to mount ten. Talk's easier than abandoning your holes for someone else to discover."

Pop turned to Sandy. "What we need to know is how you figure in this. If this T. teamed up with your friend, Grandview, we just have to trail behind you a ways and wait for them to come to us. Either that, or you hitch with us and we'll ride right out to them."

"Grandview's a madman who enjoyed torturing prisoners of war. And T. . . . he's a coward. My first priority's to get No-Neck's daughter safe to Three Forks. From there, I'm not sure. Hunting down those men doesn't appeal to me. But if they show up looking for trouble, I guess they'll find it. I don't expect to spend the rest of my life looking back to see a couple of loonies aiming their guns at me." Sandy gently pulled on his boots and eased out the front door.

Off to the east, above the canyon wall, loomed the snowcapped peaks of the Teton range. In the noon sun, the pines cast short shadows. A deep blue sky displayed drifts of puffy clouds that on occasion blocked the sun. Looking down on the now deserted meadow, Sandy did what he'd been doing at every decent-looking scene for the past five years. He mentally moved in.

You could dam up the stream and make the meadow a pond, Sandy fancied. *You could build a mill over the outlet, and a house nearby. You could enjoy the scenery, have a little peace and quiet, and still sell some lumber.*

But Sandy realized the flats belonged to everyone. No one would appreciate a claim filed here. And there weren't any buyers for lumber for several hundred miles. And Mowrey. . . .

Mowrey called him to come eat dinner.

"Someday this'll make fine cattle and lumber country," Sandy mentioned to the others inside. They nodded in agreement.

"Someday this land will settle down, real nice and peaceful," Pop interjected. "But I for one probably won't live to see the day."

Sixty miles south, two men rode the timberline.

Grandview expected his cross-country quest to end soon. He'd never been outmaneuvered by anyone in his whole life. If he wanted an army commission, he got it. If he wanted to mistreat insolent Rebel prisoners, there was no one to stand in his way. If he wanted to escape imprisonment, he did just that. And if he wanted to track down and shoot some ex-Reb corporal, he saw no reason why he couldn't.

Besides, things had gone so well. For months he'd traveled on blind hunch. Then the saloon girl at the train stop in Ogden told him about the blond newcomer who passed out in the alley. She had rolled him for nearly twelve hundred dollars. When the girl didn't accept his story as a government investigator who needed the money for evidence, he just waited. After work that night Grandview slapped her around until she handed over the money. She wouldn't dare report him to the sheriff.

Running into T. Walters was his biggest break. Now he had some direction and an extra hand. They seemed to understand each other right away. Grandview could see this episode concluding in just a few days. Then he'd ride on to San Francisco to establish himself as a proper businessman.

He stopped his horse at a large boulder and surveyed the trail far below. It was hard to distinguish faces or other marks from the timberline, but it was safe there. He turned to his companion. "I thought you said this gathering wouldn't break up for a couple more weeks."

T. watched the riders down on the trail. "I don't know why they did it different this year. But he's not down there with any of those. They're all Frenchmen—you know, Canadians."

T.'s motive for tracking Thompson paralleled Grandview's. He couldn't live with the fact of his desertion during battle. He had run away during the ambush of No-Neck, and Thompson had witnessed the whole thing. Besides, Grandview bought T. supplies and guaranteed him a hundred dollars when they completed their task. *It's like getting paid to eat cake,* T. thought.

For about the sixth time, T. reminded Grandview, "We can't just ride right up into the flats. Besides, if the trappers are thinning out, Thompson must be heading north."

Grandview coaxed his gray horse along the mountainside. "I thought you said that trail couldn't be used."

"I said it was a lousy track, but it's not impossible. If we follow Rock Creek down to Denny Meadow, we could ride the stage line and retrace the trail way before Three Forks."

Grandview snorted. "Sure, and if they travel the southern route tomorrow, we'll miss them completely. We're going right for Mud Flats. If they aren't there, then it's up the north trail."

"Hey, now, I didn't sign on to walk into a hornet's nest. Those guys—"

"Those guys are mainly old men, and most of them gone. We saw them file out of the canyon with our own eyes."

T. convinced Grandview to wait near the cliffs overlooking the canyon one more day.

Sandy packed to leave Mud Flats and head up the north trail. Branch, Bradley, Jared, and the others were going south. Montana Mudd wanted to carry his hides to Bozeman, so he offered to accompany

Sandy and Mowrey. "That can be a mean route," he warned.

Sandy wasn't sure why Mudd was so accommodating, since he still had to split supplies with him. But he consented. They gathered up seven packhorses and three riding horses. Each animal was loaded to capacity for the slow journey.

The trail narrowed as they climbed past gentle sloping grass and entered timber. Granite rocks sprinkled the landscape. The timber pines clung with tenacity to canyon walls. *A vulnerable place for a gunfight,* Sandy surmised. By instinct his eyes darted to possible vantage points.

By noon they were three thousand feet above the valley floor. They stopped beside a mountain lake to rest the horses. Mudd's mare attempted to break the string all morning, so he repacked her, putting more weight on the packhorses.

By evening they reached the rocky plateau above the canyon. They could look down on almost all the north and south trails. Nothing stirred anywhere. Then Sandy thought he detected a movement at the south end of the canyon, but he couldn't determine if something was coming or going, or if it was a mere dust storm.

A brisk wind whistled across the plateau. They all shivered, but there didn't appear to be a place to make camp for the night. Mudd led them to a sink in the middle that offered granite shelter. They quickly unpacked the animals and hobbled them as Mowrey scrounged for buffalo chips. Soon a fire smoldered.

Huddled around the smoking chips, they bundled up with buffalo robes. Mudd, as usual, did most of the talking.

"Since the rendezvous days are about gone, I've got to find me a new livelihood. Now, I hear they're needing some beef up at Silver City. Pay outrageous per head. If I had a partner, I figure we could run a couple hundred at a time. If we were to sell all our supplies and hides to Reef Buford in Three Forks, he'd stake us for the rest. The way I figure it, we could bring in a couple thousand dollars each before the snow flies this winter."

That wasn't the only scheme Mudd chattered about. However, it was the only one Sandy gave any attention. They all sounded similar. A partner with some capital was needed, one who could also work hard. As Mudd rambled on to another idea, Sandy interrupted. "Mowrey, did your mother ever give you a name? I mean, were you always just called 'Mowrey'?"

She huddled closer to the fire and gazed at Sandy. After a slight pause, she said softly, "Naw-too-pah."

"What?"

"Naw-too-pah," she said a bit louder. "The one who talks too much."

Sandy and Montana guffawed.

"And what about you, Thompson?" Mowrey rejoined. "Is your name really Sandy?"

"Naw. Would you believe Theodore Arthur Thompson? But, I've been Sandy ever since the day I was born. Now, tell me, why is it you're so set against going to Three Forks?"

"Cholera," she said with a shudder. "Many people die of the disease. The girls' clothes are all secondhand. Also, I'm too old—they'd work me like a slave. My father hoped I'd finish my schooling, but now it's too late. Besides, I have too much schooling already. How smart do I have to be to marry a buffalo hunter or brave?" She stretched the robe from her shoulders to the top of her head. "Now tell me something, Mr. Theodore Arthur Thompson, why do you get so frantic about being a husband? You don't think I'd be a good wife?"

"You'll make someone a very fine wife, I'm sure. But I have many things in my life to straighten out. A wife just doesn't fit in right now. I've already told the Lord my life needs to be simpler. Getting married definitely would not simplify it. Besides, there's the matter of love, and finding a preacher, and preparing a proper wedding. . . ."

Mowrey leaned forward. "You talk to God?"

"Uh-huh, especially when I'm staring at a fight to the death."

Mowrey looked thoughtful, then smiled and dragged her buffalo robe blanket to a sleeping place.

"You know what, Thompson?" she called back.

"Yeah, what's that?" he said, yawning.

"I think you will marry me someday."

Mudd roared.

"And do you know what I think?" Sandy replied. "I think you are Naw-too-pah—the girl who talks too much."

CHAPTER
8

Three times during the night Sandy crawled out to check noises around the plateau. The three-quarter moon tinted everything with a spooky blueness. One time the horses were restless when a distant wolf howled. Another time Mowrey tossed more wood on the fire. And just before daybreak Sandy thought for sure he heard horseshoes striking rock, but he saw nothing.

"Well, that wasn't the most peaceful night's sleep," he reported as he took a cup of coffee and sat down next to Mudd, "but it was warmer than I expected."

Mowrey handed the men some broiled meat as Sandy sighed, "One day at a time. That's all you can think about out here. Makes it hard to plan for the future."

"Yeah," Mudd said grinning, "but it makes it easy to forget the past."

It didn't take Mudd long to pack the animals. Whatever Mudd's many faults, Sandy took comfort from the fact that he'd tramped most his life through these western mountains.

The group then began the descent through the trees. Most of the morning Mudd sang a song about a muleskinner on the Santa Fe Trail, and Mowrey pouted.

Mowrey wanted to kick herself for her talk about marrying Thompson. She hit her horse harder than usual instead. *I sound like one of those bratty girls at school,* she stormed to herself.

She wasn't so sure she wanted to marry Thompson after all. Maybe he attracted her because she saw him as a convenient escape from her situation. She had no home, no one to belong to. She worried about living in a white man's town, yet she didn't relish moving in with an Indian encampment either. Neither society held much regard for a half-breed. *If I'm left at the school,* she speculated, *I'll probably run away with the first man who'll have me, white or red.*

Meanwhile, Sandy's mind raced through all the alternatives to facing Grandview. Surely such a vast land as this would be big enough to avoid an enemy from the past. There must be plenty of places to find peace and rest. However, Sandy had to admit he'd never found the circumstances of his life, whether in the East or the West, always sensible, and certainly Grandview had never proved himself reasonable.

Still, Sandy determined not to allow this man to dictate the direction of his every decision and turn. If Grandview wanted revenge, he'd have to come find him. He refused to play the hunt-or-be-hunted game.

At the meadow, Grandview encountered just a few trappers. They didn't respond well to his threats. He left with rifles pointed in his direction and decided he didn't really need their help. He had deduced by now that Thompson hadn't left on the southern route, and he wasn't in Mud Flats. Only one choice remained.

Grandview and T. climbed the canyon a distance of twenty-four hours behind Mowrey, Sandy, and Mudd. Though they could travel much faster, the going wasn't easy. Neither had ridden this way before. And once they gained the plateau, they could only guess which direction from there.

Grandview had one goal: to sneak up behind Sandy and shoot him. That was all. He didn't have to waste time worrying over how to provoke Sandy to a fair battle.

T. Walters wasn't as single-minded, but he didn't object to an ambush. T. fled Georgia before the war because he couldn't imagine himself as a soldier. He'd panned gold in New Mexico, but that was hot, dirty work. Once he had driven a herd from the Rio Grande to Kansas, then quickly gambled his money away. That was when he teamed up with Big Curly Celter. Big Curly and his friends were T's kind of people. He understood them. He knew what to expect. Grandview, however, was a different sort. The longer they rode together, the more suspicious T. was. *Once Thompson's dead,* he noted to himself, *I'd better not let Grandview out of my sight until we part company.*

By noon Sandy and company departed the plateau, winding through the timbers. At first they rode through scrub pines. By early evening tall cedars, firs, and ponderosas encircled them. They stopped at a meadow by a small creek. Abundant grass supplied the stock, and they considered a night's stay. But Sandy knew the saying—"If you think you might be having unwelcome company, never camp on the trail." He urged them on.

"But I can't repack these animals," Mudd whined.

"Why not?" Sandy asked, as he plunged in himself.

"Mowrey, you tell him he's gettin' too jumpy," Mudd pleaded.

Mowrey didn't bother. Years of traveling with No-Neck taught her to listen when a good man smelled trouble. A mile off the trail, Sandy found what he wanted. A small box canyon and cliff overhang housed the stock and their small fire.

Sandy didn't know for sure why he was so cautious. He only sensed his taut nerves. He'd been hunted before. He knew he'd sleep with one eye open and one hand on the newly acquired Winchester.

About three in the afternoon, Grandview and T. discovered the sink in the plateau's middle. They spurred their exhausted mounts on. T. was relieved when Grandview finally stopped at the first tall pines for the evening's camp.

Around the fire, Grandview talked about a trading company he'd started in San Francisco. He even offered T. a position. T. didn't reply.

About two in the morning, T. awakened with the butt of Grandview's rifle against his shoulder. The ex-captain was not only awake, but dressed to ride.

"Hey, what's going on?"

"Time to hit. We can catch 'em before daylight," Grandview commanded.

"But, it's dark as pitch. . . ."

"What do you mean? There's a near full moon. The trail's well-lit. Come on, we're wasting time."

T. held his ground. "And what if I say no?"

"Nobody says no to me when my hand's on a trigger."

T. mounted.

It wasn't as easy as Grandview projected. Tall tree shadows blocked the way, and any movements caused the horses to pull up. Still, they gained territory. Neither said a word. The wind and trickling creek tried to caress the forest with gentle sounds.

As the sky tranformed from black to gray, they entered a tiny meadow. "There's been more than one rider here," Grandview commented.

T. agreed. "Since this one wears moccasins, I'd surmise the Indian girl's still with him. But I can't tell if he's got heavy riders or a string. Too dark yet. Let's wait till it lightens some more."

But Grandview waited for nothing. He lit a fire and torched a branch for a better view. He concluded that Sandy and the girl traveled alone. Then he used the branch to find the direction off the trail they'd headed down.

Sandy spotted the branch torch. He shook Mowrey and Mudd. "Someone's at the meadow," he cautioned.

"Could be trappers passing through," Mudd commented, "although it's hardly the time of day for it. Looks like they're searching for something."

"Mowrey," Sandy ordered, "take this rifle and go to the mouth of the canyon. Don't let anyone go in there and run the stock. Mudd, if your legs'll hold out, climb to the top of the overhang and lie flat. Should be a good view from there."

"A *grand* view, maybe?" he hooted. "Now, remember, partner, I never pack a gun."

Sandy spat. "How's about starting today?"

"Nope. Made me a promise to the good Lord that I wouldn't never do it. He'd have to see me through another way."

"Well, you're not opposed to using that pig-sticker, are you?" Thompson growled.

"Oh, I'll use it. You can bet on that," Mudd called as he climbed the cliff.

"And where will you hide?" Mowrey questioned before she stole away.

"I don't aim to hide at all," Sandy told her.

"That girl won't run. She'll fight," T. warned Grandview as they stalked their animals toward the canyon.

"So, you'll shoot the girl," Grandview said. "And I'll get Thompson. Or, if you'd rather—"

"I'll do my fair share of shooting. Just make sure this is the right camp. I don't want to shoot up every camp in sight trying to find this man."

Sandy didn't know who was approaching. He didn't know how many. And he didn't know if they intended to march the hill or circumvent them. He built a fire, then sauntered away from it next to a boulder about seventy feet away. He counted on a massive pine to protect him from snipers behind. The rock and Winchester guarded the front. Nothing left to do but wait.

• • •

Just before daylight, Grandview spotted the fire. He surveyed the area and saw buffalo robes, packs, saddles, and assorted gear, but no people. Grandview decided to sit awhile. Someone would show sooner or later.

Sandy made the first move. He feared Mowrey and Mudd would grow too restless and expose themselves. And the long silence revealed the less than honorable motives of the approachers. It also indicated a lack of planning. That gave Sandy an edge. He pulled his brown hat low on the back of his head to cover the blond hair. Then he eased back into camp with an exaggerated limp, hoping that whoever was out there would be confused about his identity.

Halfway to the fire, Sandy had second thoughts about his idea. But it was too late. He crouched down for an empty coffeepot and pretended to pour coffee. Loudly he drawled east toward a patch of woods, "Honey-bun, you all 'bout through out there? We needs to get breakfast started before the young'uns stir."

Grandview tightened the trigger, then hesitated. "That him?" he quizzed T.

"Can't tell, but surely no one'd travel out here with a family."

Once more Grandview stalled. He had no qualms about shooting someone in the back, but he suddenly had a great desire to let Sandy know

142

that it was Robert Grandview doing the shooting. He wanted to watch his eyes before he sent him to the grave.

Grandview signaled T. to approach from the east. Then he strolled up to the clearing. The man huddled under a robe at the fire. "Mister! Don't make a move, or you're a dead man!"

Sandy recognized the voice this time. No mistake like on the train at Ogden. Sandy slowly turned, head lowered, and clutching the robe. "Say, we don't got nothin' worth stealing, lessen it be these here buffalo robes."

Grandview lowered his rifle to the ground in front of Sandy. That's when he heard the sound few men in the West treasured—the click of two cocked pistols. The robe slid off, exposing the .44 in one hand, and the Rigdon and Ansley .36 in the other. "Grandview, if you so much as twitch, I'll blow your head off. Drop the rifle!"

"Thompson, you son of a—"

"Save your praises, Grandview." He watched as the rifle slid to the dirt. He kept another eye out for T. "So, Yankee justice set you free? Why didn't you stay back east where everybody hated you? No reason to come west and make more enemies."

"You were always an insolent Rebel, Thompson. My only regret is in not finishing you when I had the chance."

"But you thought you *had* finished me,

remember? I carry a scar as a souvenir. A brave man you are, Grandview. Tie a man's hands over his head and slice him with his own sword." Sandy glanced again at the woods. "Grandview, tell T. that he'd better make his first shot count."

"You think I need help to kill you?" Grandview sneered.

"It sure looks like you could use a right hand at the moment. Now, turn very slowly and call him in. Tell him to step out into the clear."

"You're a fool, Thompson. You'll never get out of this." But he did call T.

T. had been a second-string player most of his life. He always followed someone else's orders, but that didn't mean he was dumb. He assessed the layout of this situation and realized the advantage of the overhang lookout. While the drama unfolded below, he circled the camp and startled an engrossed Mudd, "I'm up here, Thompson, right by your friend. I've got a cocked pistol to the head, too." Mudd hadn't had time to even draw his knife.

Grandview felt a sudden surge of the old power. "It's a draw, Thompson. If I die, your friend dies, and you shoot it out with T., who has the better position. I suggest you let T. and me walk out of here and we settle this another day."

"You've got to be kidding. T. doesn't bother me. He's a coward and a dead man. Right now dozens of trappers comb these hills looking for him because of No-Neck's murder. When they catch him, he'll wish he'd been captured by Apaches." Sandy raised his voice. "How much he paying you, T.?"

No reply. "How much pay?" Sandy repeated.

"A hundred dollars," T. said with a tense edge.

"Have you seen the money yet, T.? Answer me that. Have you seen a single cent?" Sandy goaded.

"I don't pay until a job's done," Grandview snorted.

"T.!" Thompson yelled, "I'm going to do you another favor. Two weeks ago I had a clear shot at your back. You do remember, don't you? After you threw down your gun and deserted your friends. I'm not kidding about the trappers. They know what you look like and they see it as their God-given duty to track you to settle the score for No-Neck. But they headed south. If you were to jump on your horse right now and cut a figure nine for Canada, you just might live to a feisty old age."

T. seemed to consider the option, and Mudd grabbed for his knife. T. quickly regained his control and kicked the weapon from Mudd's hand. The old trapper struggled to his feet. T.'s two-handed slam to the face tumbled him over the side of the granite overhang. He crashed to the floor below and didn't move.

Sandy turned, and Grandview kicked burning embers at him. As Sandy frantically brushed them away, Grandview dove for his rifle and into the forest. A shot was fired in Sandy's direction. Sandy rushed to the overhang, but from there he realized he was a ready target for ricochet bullets. Every shot could bounce six times. He couldn't even check on Mudd, who still slumped on the ground.

With the first shot Mowrey left the stock to come investigate. Her rifle had been trained on Grandview, but Mudd's fall diverted her. She realized that if T. raised up from his low place on the rock, she had a clear shot at him. But if he stayed there, he could easily pick her off as she left the canyon. She considered stampeding the stock, but feared the horses would run over Mudd. She knew better than to join Sandy in his vulnerable location. The only alternative was to find a way out of the canyon, ring around T., and surprise him.

Mowrey tried to slip away as the men below watched and waited for someone to make a move.

Thousands of years of water erosion had carved steep walls on all three sides of the boxed-in canyon. Over the past decades scrub pines had attempted to grow along red walls. Mowrey saw them as her only chance. She tied the rifle to her back with a piece of rawhide, then pulled herself up, one tree at a time. She dragged herself across the rock wall, each inch a struggle. Her beads ripped loose, her dress wore thin, the frayed tassels shredded, and red clay plastered the rest.

She reached for a pine. It gave away. She tumbled backward fifteen feet but was saved by another tree. Her dress tore from the high back to the waist. Blood flowed from her forehead as she crashed against an outcropped ledge. Yet she kept on. At this point, it was even harder to go back. She had never given up on anything before.

Secure in his perch on top the overhang, T. tried not to think about Sandy's words. But the growing uneasiness haunted him. It made sense. If the trappers knew he'd been part of No-Neck's killing, then these mountains were the worst place to be, no matter what happened below. But he hesitated to flee another battle.

He didn't relish a coward's reputation.

He decided he would head for Canada as soon as Sandy was finished. *Or better yet,* he thought, *why not shoot Grandview? Make it look like they shot each other, and take the goods of both.*

Meanwhile, Sandy devised an escape. If he could manufacture a diversion at one side of the entrance, he might dive and roll quick enough out the other side to the woods. Once there, he and Mowrey would have an even chance. The old hat on the end of a stick might work, but he would still be on the wrong side of the cave. And he would still gamble with ricochets. *If I could only raise the stick from a safe distance. . . .*

He found an appropriate stick at the back of the cave, and looked for a rope. He rummaged through the supplies they had tossed in the cave the night before. All he could find was the pair of beaded moccasins he had worn in the fight with Little Wolf. Sandy removed the rawhide laces and tied them together. They measured about ten feet—not quite the distance he wanted, but better than nothing.

He put his props in place, then anticipated the right moment. If the hat raised correctly, and if Grandview looked that way, and if T. didn't . . . and if Sandy got a good running leap, he might make it.

Mowrey collapsed at the canyon top. As she gasped for breath, she peered back down the sheer ascent. After a brief rest, she ventured around the canyon's edge toward T. When she spied him, she resisted the urge to fire at once. She feared that in her condition she wouldn't be accurate. Crouched behind a rock, she checked her rifle. She noticed the slightly bent front sights, then propped the Winchester on the rock.

A ground squirrel scurried through the clearing. Sandy swung up the hat. He heard Grandview's rifle cock and fire. Sandy lunged for tree cover in the opposite direction. Several bullets from two different weapons hit the dirt around him. Lying flat behind the tree, he calculated he had landed right between the two gunmen. If he rose to fire in one direction, he would be a perfect mark for the other.

He glanced to the rear for any sign of T. He could hear Grandview advance in the woods. A reflection from T.'s direction caught his eye. "You still up there, Walters?" he hollered. "Thought you'd be in Canada by now."

"Where in the world is Mowrey?" he muttered in a sweat under his breath. He kept his eye on the forest as he bantered with T. "Tell you what—if you'll throw down your gun and ride out of here, I'll make sure the Indian girl with the rifle behind you holds her fire," he bluffed. Sandy thought he heard a rustling of movement from above. "Look, T., you know she's with me. And you know she's not afraid to shoot. You should have seen Big Curly at the bottom of that ravine after she unloaded No-Neck's Sharps. After all, she's his daughter. She's got just cause to shoot you."

T. Walters whirled around in time to face the rifle barrel twenty-five yards above him. His rifle never reached above his knees. Mowrey's first bullet hit his throat, the second caught his chest. "This one's taken care of. What about the other?" Mowrey yelled down.

"Shouldn't take long from up there . . . like

shooting squirrels in a cage," Sandy shouted back.

Sandy fired a shot in Grandview's direction. No one returned fire. "See anything?" Sandy called to Mowrey.

"No . . . wait . . . down the hill . . . a rider!"

Sandy pursued on foot and discovered Grandview's footprints. He found where Grandview mounted his horse and spooked T.'s. His retreating figure had just crossed the creek and raced through the trees. Sandy fired a shot in frustration. He knew by the time he returned for his horse, Grandview would be well hidden. He swung around in a fury to check on Mowrey and Mudd.

Mowrey scooted off the cliff as he reached the clearing. Sandy gaped at the muddy, bloody figure. "Did you wrestle a bear?" he asked with some gentleness.

"I did what had to be done," she replied with no smile.

"I've got to check on Mudd. You get down to the creek and wash yourself. And look in my saddlebag, on the left side. There's a present for you. I was saving it for Three Forks, but it looks like you need it now."

Mudd, unconscious, bled from a gash above his right ear. Sandy dragged him to the cave's edge, then bolstered him against the wall. He washed out the wound with some of Mudd's whiskey, then wet the bandana and squeezed it over Mudd's mouth.

The old trapper flinched. He began to mumble, "Stampede . . . stampede . . . must be ten thousand buffalo. . . . I couldn't turn them . . . they kept comin' and comin' . . . my head, oh, my head. . . ."

"Here, drink this," Sandy prompted. "You deserve to have your gut as rotted as your customers. And there's no stampede. You took a bad fall, that's all. Just relax. I think you've got enough padding to keep from breaking any bones."

Still dazed, Mudd jabbered on. "I'm a goner, I'm a goner for sure. The whole herd's comin' this way. Oh, Lord, here I come. 'The Lord is my shepherd; I shall not want. . . .'"

Sandy shook the mountain man. "Mudd! Mudd!"

But he only ranted louder. "'He maketh me to lie down in green pastures. He—'"

Sandy began to get that old haunting feeling. "Mudd! Mudd!"

"'Yea, though I walk through the valley of the shadow. . . .' Oh, Lord, I see heaven . . . I'm surrounded by angels. . . . You didn't forget me, did you, Lord?"

Montana Mudd reached out for something beyond Sandy, then passed out again.

Sandy felt Mudd's pulse. Then he started as he sensed something behind him.

A few feet away stood a freshly scrubbed Mowrey dressed in blue gingham, with flowing, unbraided hair. Highlights from the sun played in her hair. Except for the barely visible gash, she looked like an angel in the wilderness.

"Well," Sandy said, beaming, "I'll bet this is the first time your beauty caused a man to faint."

"But not the last time, Theodore Arthur Thompson." Then she added shyly, "I hope it's not the last time."

CHAPTER
9

Mowrey felt strange in the new blue dress. She hadn't worn anything but buckskin for years. Besides, soft, dainty clothes like this didn't last long in the mountains or prairies. But it was all she had for now.

"Are we going after Grandview?" she asked Sandy.

"No, not now," Sandy replied while rubbing the back of his neck. "He's too far ahead of us, and Mudd needs attention."

Mowrey led the stock around, and the two of them packed the supplies. They cinched down the last animal when Mudd called out, "Well, did we get 'em, partner?" Mudd cradled his head as he searched for the nearest bottle of whiskey.

"Best we could with you falling off the cliff and sleeping through it all," Sandy chided.

"Fall? I didn't fall. I was bushwhacked, I was. Did you get them both?"

"I didn't get either of them. Mowrey shot T., and Grandview escaped."

Montana Mudd staggered over to the pack animals and began to retie the whole string. "You didn't go after him?"

"He was long gone before I could reach a horse. Besides, I had to doctor you, that's what," Sandy countered.

"Shoot, it'd take more than a dive on the rocks to do me in," Mudd boasted.

"I don't know. For a time there even you thought it was the end of the trail. You quoted from the Good Book."

"I did? Well, it don't hurt for a man to have a little religion. Ain't that right, Mowrey?"

"I think a lot of religion's better than a little," she replied in her schoolteacher tone.

"You a missionary Indian?" Mudd pried.

"I'd be happy to explain my faith to you," Mowrey replied.

"It ain't Sunday yet," Mudd rebutted.

When Mudd announced he was ready, they plodded down the mountain, watching out for Grandview at every turn, but his tracks showed him still hurrying along the hill.

All Grandview wanted right now was a dozen good men who'd obey orders and ride with him.

He had always considered himself a commander, a leader who others naturally followed.

The high mountain trail crossed a large river, then joined a wider trail to a massive meadow below. Grandview paused at the junction and debated. To the west, riders advanced. He hid out of sight as they cantered into view. It looked as though Robert Grandview lucked out again. He rode out to meet them.

Still wearing the army sergeant's uniform he had stolen in his escape from prison, he appealed in his best official tone. "Gentlemen, I'm Sergeant Grandview. I'm on a special investigation after fugitives. One Eastern criminal's been spotted on this trail, and I hope to bring him in. I'd like to swear you in as assistants. How many will go with me?"

The spokesman of the group rode up close and looked him over. "You say you're a sergeant?"

"That's right. I'm working out of Fort Laramie," Grandview lied.

"Funny you should travel alone," the man said.

"My partner was shot up near the plateau. That's why I need civilian help," he said as calmly as he could.

"Partner? And what's your partner's name?" the man quizzed.

"Walters . . . T. Walters. A good man, too. But I'm afraid he's dead. So, gentlemen, if those who're willing will raise their right arm—"

"Whoa, wait just a minute, Sergeant." He looked back at the group. "Just what do we get out of this? We expect a little gratuity for all this patriotic pride. What if this man's got a crew with him?"

"All right, I'll pay each of you twenty dollars to ride with me just for today. If we don't get my man, you can still ride away with the money."

"Tell you what, Sergeant. You pay us twenty-five dollars each right now, before we ride, and you got yourself a deal."

"I don't pay until the job's done," Grandview informed them.

"And we don't ride until we get paid," the leader retorted.

"Sure, and how do I know you'd ride with me?" Grandview countered.

The group of men murmured.

"I said we'd ride with you until you found this here fugitive. Now, are you calling me a liar?" the leader charged.

Grandview, poker-faced, dismounted and pulled out a sachel of coins. "Gentlemen, I've got a twenty-dollar gold piece for any who'll ride up the trail with me right now. And there's another if we capture the man. Now, who's coming?"

The man pulled off his hat and wiped his brow. "I reckon we could all use a little jingle. What do you say, boys? Shall we ride with him?"

They all quickly agreed. Soon, eleven riders, with

Grandview at the head, plowed up the mountain. Grandview showed them a good site for an ambush, and ordered, "Hide in the rocks, all of you!"

No one moved.

Grandview called their leader over. "Look here—"

"Branch. The name's Branch."

"Branch, your men need to do what I tell them," he fumed.

Branch talked nice and easy. "Just relax, Sergeant. We've got our own plans. Pop, you relieve Mr. Grandview of his guns, then tie him to that tree. Jared, you and Mike get a fire going. Let's have a little hot grub prepared for Sandy and the others."

"What?" Grandview yelled.

"And Pop, stick your bandana in his mouth so we don't have to listen to that awful hollering."

Sandy spied out the encampment below. He recognized Pop from clear across the ravine. The three relaxed for the first time in days as they rode into camp.

"Ooooweee! Mowrey never looked prettier!" Pop whistled. Mowrey blushed as she dismounted and joined the others.

"What happened to you?" Jared asked Mudd.

"He fought a granite floor, and lost," Sandy explained. "We left T. dead, halfway up the mountain. But Grandview got away. Headed in this direction. What are you old trappers doing around here? We thought you rode south."

"We did go south," Branch said, "but some Frenchmen reported two men riding timber. We figured from our position it'd be better to cut across Denny Meadow and up river to the trail junction. We hoped to be of some help, but I guess the shootin's done."

"Unless Grandview wants to make another attempt," Sandy said.

"Now, that reminds me," Pop spoke up. "Sandy, I'm wonderin' if you'd let me see that pistol of yours?"

"Sure, you ought to get yourself one—"

"And, if you don't mind, would you walk over to the river with me? There's someone we'd like you to see. We promised him you wouldn't be packin' an iron." Pop led the way.

Sandy let out a low whistle. "Grandview? Tied to a tree? Why the disarming?"

"Well," Branch began, "Grandview hired us to capture you. Gave us twenty dollars each in advance, and offered another twenty on delivery. What do you say, Thompson, are you captured?"

"Oh, yes, definitely. I'm captured. You should collect what's yours."

High-pitched murmurs sputtered from behind the bandana as Wayne Jared counted out the coins from Grandview's supply. Then, they returned to camp.

"Now that we've been properly paid, I suppose you can have your hardware back." Pop handed Sandy the .36. They swapped stories in the shade and ate beans and jerky.

Then, Branch cleared his throat and turned to Sandy. "What happens now?"

"I assume you're talking about Grandview. Well, it's a bit complicated. I'm not for shooting a man tied to a tree. But I can't haul him to a sheriff because he'd tell about my withdrawal back in Virginia. I suppose we could just leave him there. Or you could give me three days lead, then do whatever you want."

Wayne Jared interrupted. "I think we've got us a contest brewin' here. You and Mudd and Mowrey get on your way. The rest of us were set for a two-month chase anyway, so we're in no hurry. We'll just set up here until we think of a fittin' repose for the sergeant. The one with the best answer gets a keg of Mudd's rotgut."

"Yeah, and the one with the second-best solution gets two kegs!" Ian, the Scotsman, rolled the whole camp in laughter.

By nightfall the three reached the foot of the mountain and began to cross the valley floor toward Three Forks. They made camp on the Madison and prepared to reach town late the next day.

Sandy assumed the Grandview conflict wasn't over, but he did sense a reprieve. He took time to sit against a cottonwood and glory in a sunset. *Out here in the West you can see for miles with no obstructions to God's creation,* he mused. *You can anticipate new beginnings, no matter which way you look. No battle-scarred cities, no congestion, no manmade noise or confusion. Just wide open spaces. . . .*

Sandy sighed as he drank in the vastness. The rugged peaks stretched thousands of feet above the valleys. The year-round snowcaps, roaring rivers, and lush grasslands spread out as far as the eye could see. Jagged canyons, primeval forests, and wildlife as free as the clouds above lured the restless wanderer.

The sun slipped behind the Bitterroots, shading the expansive river and pass. That same area had beckoned Lewis and Clark over fifty years earlier. *Now, those would have been the days,* Sandy reflected. *Hiking to the Pacific with Captain Clark. Forging your way up the Yellowstone with Coulter. Crossing the Rockies with Bridger. Explorers, adventurers, men not content to stand still, who resisted conformity to the world around them.*

Sandy felt he understood their spirit well. He was carved from the same timber. *Just fifty years too late.*

But a big country like this could surely still breed big ideas. Somehow, the West of 1870 still spawned endless possibilities. For Sandy, it might be a cattle ranch, or maybe a lumber mill. After all, the lumber business was a family tradition.

Family—that stirred up powerful memories for Sandy. His eyes rested on the yellow glow left from the western Montana sun, but his mind relived the Shenandoah Valley.

"It's not worth dying for!" Those words had spewed from his father. "Slavery's not worth dying for, but defending your home is!"

Sandy and his brother, Ralph Wayne, joined the Confederate army only after war had been declared. Union troops soon gathered at the entry to their valley. He could not allow an army to destroy his homeland without a struggle.

Early in the campaign, their spirits high, they expected a quick settlement. But weeks dragged into years, the issues forgotten. They wanted to defeat the Yankees at any cost. Twice his own troops destroyed his hometown while driving out the enemy. After the war, nothing remained. No farm, no horses, no mill, no Ralph Wayne, no Mom and Dad.

However, he was out west now. This land shouted, "Give it another try! Give it your best!" Sandy, like thousands before him, responded to that challenge.

"Do you plan to just sit and stare all night?" Mowrey startled him back to the present.

"Sometimes sitting and staring's the most important thing a man can do," Sandy replied.

"It all seems peaceful this time of the night," she continued. "Deceptive, isn't it?"

"Yeah, all of life's that way," Sandy said, staring out at the night. "Someday it will be different."

"What do you mean?"

"Well, maybe one day somebody will come along and draw the line. You know, call a halt to needless violence. No more ambushes, no more shots in the back, no more scalping. Then this country will be as peaceful all the time as it is right now."

She smiled. "It will take a lot more than just one man drawing the line to tame this land."

"Well, maybe so. But it will all begin when one man draws the line and says, 'That's it.' "

Mowrey said nothing for a moment. Then she ventured, "The other day you said you sometimes talk to God. Is that true?"

Sandy scratched the dirt with his fingers. "Sure, everybody talks to God when they're desperate enough."

"Well, I talk to God even when I'm not scared," she said in a distant tone. "But I don't always know if he hears me. I'm going with you tomorrow to Three Forks. But I sure have prayed that I won't have to stay at that school."

Sandy started to reply when Mudd lumbered up. He flopped down next to Mowrey. "Say, did I ever tell you about the time I tried to ride a bighorn sheep?"

Neither Sandy or Mowrey encouraged him, but Montana Mudd rambled on.

They reached Three Forks about dark the next day. Since this wasn't the time for trading or for finding the Margaret Cady School for Wayward Indian Girls, they camped outside town.

Sandy and Mowrey both felt the awkwardness. Now that the parting was so close on them, it seemed they'd known each other much longer than a mere three weeks. Mowrey, and even Mudd, began to have the feel of family to Sandy. He assumed the girl's comments about marriage had been excuses to avoid Three Forks. To him marriage meant sturdy farm houses, clean white sheets, and homemade blueberry pie cooling in a window—things he wanted someday but not now.

Tonight's burnt buffalo chips reminded him how far short that dream was from reality. Just the same, it finally hit him that leaving Mowrey would be almost as difficult as leaving home. He dreaded tomorrow, so he coped by ignoring her.

Mowrey didn't notice. Her thoughts swirled around the school. Would Yellow Flower still be there? Though she was two years younger than Mowrey, they had been close. She remembered their promise to each other that if they hadn't married by age sixteen, they would run away to the East and find themselves some rich men. Even then they knew that was an impossible pursuit, both being half-breeds. Besides, they knew nothing about the East except what they had read in library books.

She smiled to herself. Now, an Eastern man had found her. But this Sandy Thompson lived too much in the past. *He's not happy,* she concluded. *He misses the joy of today by dwelling on the sorrow of yesterday. Well, if this school isn't any better than it was before, I'll just walk away and be free at last. No father, and no Thompson, to lead me around.* But her throat caught in a lump at the thought.

Sandy outlined the day. He and Mudd would carry the supplies and hides into Buford's. Then, they would go to the cattle yard to check on deals for several hundred head to drive to Silver City— one of Mudd's schemes. Sandy had agreed to go with him, if he would promise to bathe and shave. After lunch, Mowrey would be off to school.

"We'll stay in town several days to make sure you're settled in," Sandy assured Mowrey.

"I don't mean to sound ungrateful," she said, "but I'm old enough to care for myself, as you've both witnessed. The quicker you two are gone, the sooner I can get my life in order."

"Well, isn't that a schoolgirl attitude for you!" Mudd chortled. "She sure told you off."

Sandy stood with his mouth open. The more he learned about Mowrey, the more she surprised him. Sometimes she played the subservient Indian maid. Other times she sounded more like a girl named Cynthia Jo Claymore back in Virginia. Cynthia Jo never subserved to anyone.

At Buford's they gleaned both good and bad news. The storekeeper offered them eighteen hundred dollars for their hides and supplies. Also, a dire need existed for cattle up in the Owyhee Mountains. But all the town's cattle were taken. Mudd and Sandy would have to wait for another drive to reach town. Also, it could cost them anywhere between twelve and twenty dollars a head for the beef once they got them to their destination.

They reconsidered the cattle business as they walked to the Emporium. Mudd hadn't bathed yet, but neither had Sandy. Only Mowrey looked presentable. But they ignored the stares of the finer citizenry of Three Forks. They ordered large cuts of beef, plenty of rich milk, and fresh fruit. Mowrey wanted eggs, too.

They had just begun to eat when they overheard a loud conversation at the table next to them. "Jordan, since when does the Emporium serve whiskey traders and breeds?"

The owner tried to quiet him. "I'm sure they'll leave soon, Mr. Whittley. Would you like another table?"

The heavy man continued his complaint. "No, sir, I want to know if you intend to serve breeds. The next thing you know, every thieving

Blackfoot and Gros Ventre will be lining up for grub. You certainly won't see the likes of me anymore."

"I'm not sure what I can do, Mr. Whittley. A customer is a—"

The big man slammed the table. "There must be a law against serving breeds. You could throw her out in the street, and I'm sure the sheriff could find some reason to jail those drifters. That's why we have law and order." He yelled over to Sandy, "Hey, squaw man, you and that Indian bunkmate of yours are not welcome here. It's to your definite advantage to leave at once." He then stood, exposing a pistol tucked into his belt. His hand rested on the grip.

Sandy rose, too, his temples pulsing. "Let me tell you something. My gold's as good as yours, and probably more honorably acquired. You, sir, have just insulted this lady's honor. Where I come from there's only two courses of action. Either you draw that pistol, or you come here on your knees and apologize."

"Gentlemen, gentlemen, please, not in the Emporium," Jordan pleaded.

"I am not now, nor ever, about to apologize to any foul-smelling squaw," George Whittley huffed.

"Then I suggest your guests move back from the table. I'm packing a .36 that'll leave most of your brains plastered against that white linen tablecloth," Sandy taunted. He tried to calm himself.

"You got a wife? Then, I suggest you tell her good-bye before you lift that weapon from your pants."

By now, most of the patrons clung to the safety of the far walls or the sidewalk outside. Jordan sent one of the cooks for the sheriff.

George Whittley found himself about two steps down the trail farther than he intended. The thought of this gang eating in the same room repulsed him. But he knew he wasn't the world's fastest gun. Even so, he'd never apologize to an Indian. With great pomp he turned to leave the Emporium. "You have disturbed my meal enough. I'll tolerate no more of this."

"Mister!" Sandy barked. "Either draw that gun or kneel to the lady. One or the other. And I trust the gentlemen at the door believe in the same code I do." Sandy speculated that this obnoxious man had rubbed others wrong, too. A couple of six-footers blocked Whittley's exit. The tallest of them said, "If you've got a point to prove, Whittley, go ahead and prove it."

"The lady's waiting," Sandy snapped.

Though Sandy had been in the West just a few months, he didn't worry about outdrawing the man across from him. For three war years he fought alongside the fastest draws in south Texas, the Baldwin brothers of San Angelo. They took delight in teaching a green kid from Virginia the Texas draw.

"I never apologized to any breed." Whittley grabbed for the ivory handle. Sandy's .36 stood cocked and pointed at the man's temple before Whittley's pistol had barely left his belt and pointed at the floor. He dropped his gun.

"You've got thirty seconds to get over here and start talking. There are plenty of witnesses. One . . . two . . . three . . . four. . . ."

Whittley slowly shuffled toward Mowrey, who still sat at her table.

"Seventeen . . . eighteen . . . nineteen. . . ."

"I'm sorry . . . ," Whittley stammered.

"Not good enough, mister. I said, *on your knees!* Twenty-four . . . twenty-five . . . twenty-six. . . ."

"Good Lord, man, quit the counting. Look, I'm on my knees." Sweat poured down Whittley as he tried to loosen his collar.

"Wait just a minute." Sandy turned to the door. "Would you boys invite the other guests back in? Since they heard the insult, too, I want them to be sure to hear the apology as well."

A group crowded back into the dining hall. "Say it again," Sandy ordered, as he held the cocked .36 right behind the man's earlobe.

"I'm sorry," Whittley mumbled, without looking up.

"Look her in the eye and say it louder. Say, 'Young lady, please forgive me for casting unfounded dispersion on your virtue.' "

With more than fifty people looking on, George

Whittley repeated the words that would haunt him for years to come. He didn't even notice that Sandy holstered his pistol, or that Sheriff Bob Roy Wiley now stood in the audience.

Mowrey accepted the apology, and they sat down to finish their meal. Whittley stormed out in a hurry, amidst a flurry of many hoots and hollers.

Two of the men who had blocked the doorway marched to their table. "You going to arrest him, Sheriff?" asked the taller man.

"The way I hear it, there's no call to. Besides, I don't like arresting folks that come from the green hills of the Shenandoah."

Sandy's face creased into a wide grin at the familiar face and voice. "Bob Roy? Bob Roy Wiley, is that really you?"

"It ain't General Lee. Man, it's great to see you. How long you been out here?"

"Just got to town today. But I left Virginia a year ago." Sandy still couldn't believe he was talking to this old school chum. "What in the world is a Reb like you doing as sheriff?"

"Out here they don't much care where you're from, just so you do the job. I came out west straightways after we called it quits in the Louisiana swamps. Been sheriff here almost two years."

"Hey, I want you to meet my friends. Mowrey's the daughter of the legendary No-Neck Mowrey, and this one's Montana Mudd."

"You two hitched up?"

"Oh, no. Just friends. I owe her father a favor."

"Didn't mean to be nosy. I'm a married man myself. In fact, we have a little one coming along any day now." Bob Roy pulled up a chair. "Melissa and I would be proud to have you all stay with us awhile."

"I wouldn't pass up Southern hospitality in any country," Sandy responded. "Say, did you find a Southern girl out here in this wilderness?"

"Are there any other kind?" Bob Roy laughed as he slapped Sandy's back.

Mowrey visibly squirmed as a well-dressed man burst up to the table. "I hate to interrupt, Sheriff, but I'd like to introduce myself to this newcomer." He tipped his hat. "I'm the publisher of the Three Forks *Examiner*, and I'd sure like to feature the ruckus with Whittley in tomorrow's edition. Can I get some names? Some details?"

Bob Roy stood. "This is Mowrey, Montana Mudd, and Sandy Thompson, lately from Winchester, Virginia. He held the title of best shot and most eligible bachelor in the Shenandoah . . . that is, next to his brother, Ralph Wayne. By the way, how is Ralph Wayne?"

"He's dead," Sandy said with a frown.

"Well, uh, I'd like to use your names in my article," the publisher prattled on.

"I guess so," Sandy said with some uncertainty. "Hey, Bob Roy, is this Whittley guy the kind of fellow who waits outside in the dark for you? Should I be checking the alleys while we're here?"

"You're coming home with me tonight. By tomorrow the *Examiner* will disclose the whole story. My guess is Whittley will find some excuse to leave town for a time. Now, finish up, and come to my office. I want you to meet my Melissa. She's as sweet as she can be, and straight from South Carolina." Bob Roy bowed to Mowrey. "Can we count on all three of you for dinner?"

"I'll decline, thank you," Mudd said with as much politeness as he could muster. "I've got some old friends to look up. However, I will take you up on a Southern supper, if you still have a mind to invite an old mountain man. Why, I'll even clean up."

"You've got it. We'll set fried chicken and the lightest sweet bread this side of Savannah. Just you and Mowrey, then?"

"Well, I promised her father I'd bring her to the Margaret Cady School. We're going there now."

"Don't count on it," Bob Roy replied. "You're about two years too late. The school closed down."

Mowrey gasped, then beamed at Sandy. "Was it smallpox?"

The sheriff continued, "No, I think cholera did them in, not to mention a few other problems. The whole works closed tighter than a drum about a month before I was sworn in. Now they use the old brick building as a . . . well, shall I say, it's a home for soiled doves."

Mowrey felt as though she had just been released from prison. "The school's a bordello!" she exclaimed with a chuckle. "A sporting house!"

Sandy didn't know what to say or do.

"I'll let Melissa know you'll be staying a few days," said the sheriff as he turned to leave. "It's a cinch you'll need time to sort things out."

Mudd pushed his chair away from the table and excused himself. "Got a date with destiny," he announced. "By the way, where's the nearest bath-house?"

Sandy slowly sipped another cup of hot coffee. Mowrey stared out the window.

"Well, Mr. Theodore Arthur Thompson, what will you do with me now?" She didn't dare look at him.

"I'm not sure," Sandy answered. "But I have eliminated a few choices."

"Oh? Which ones?"

"I'm not going to shoot you, and I'm not going to marry you!" He touched her shoulder. "Come on, let's buy a present for Bob Roy's future little one, then go visiting. We'll do our figuring later."

CHAPTER
10

The closing of the Margaret Cady School for Wayward Indian Girls immensely complicated the life of Sandy Thompson. This was to have been the last stop of this wild West saga. Tomorrow had promised fewer encumbrances, new horizons. His agenda included a business deal or two, further journeys west, and the eventual trip to California to reunite with his long-lost sister.

Now he had a female to care for. Or did he? After all, he'd kept his promise to No-Neck. And Mowrey was by no means a helpless young thing. But could he just dump her on the streets of Three Forks?

He recalled the mention of relatives in Oregon—that might be the solution. He would ride through the Idaho Territory with her to search for her relatives. That thought eased his mind a bit as they strolled over to the Wileys' home.

Bob Roy tidied up some papers as Mowrey and Sandy entered his tiny office. The sheriff of Three Forks didn't serve the most prestigious position in the West, but it was respectable. He earned fifteen dollars a week, and the city provided a house and all the beef the Wileys could eat.

172

While Mowrey scanned the wanted posters, Sandy looked his old childhood chum over. He could see Bob Roy had always been the sheriff type. As a kid he had enforced the rules of every game. He organized the teams, made sure everyone played fairly, and made peace when conflicts arose. He served well as lieutenant in the Confederate army. And he looked so natural with a badge.

"So tell me," Bob Roy said, as they strolled to his house, "where's Sandy Thompson headed? Weren't you the man who was going to discover new worlds? Climb distant mountains? Build bigger buildings? Travel farther than any of us? Say, Mowrey, did he tell you about his favorite fantasy? Sandy used to tell us he was going to have a whole mountain range named after himself. Not one measly mountain, mind you, but a whole sweep of them."

"Come on, Bob Roy, if you start telling childhood secrets, I'll have to tell your Melissa about you and Sedalia Strathmore."

"Hey, no you don't . . . or I'll lock you up in a cell so fast. . . ."

Both men laughed deeper than they had in years. It felt so good to Sandy to be reminded of more pleasant episodes of the past.

Melissa greeted them at the door of the small white clapboard house. She wore a soft yellow dress, freshly ironed and starched in the true

Southern style. For a moment Sandy imagined he stood on the great front porch of the Wiley farm, waiting to attend the senior ball.

Mowrey and Melissa became instant friends. Their differences enhanced their pleasure of one another's company. Mowrey assumed her quiet nature while she marveled at Melissa's musical drawl.

Around the table Sandy approached his idea of driving cattle to Silver City. "Well, you're just the kind of man that could do it," Bob Roy encouraged. "But it's a tough drive. Those southern Idaho plains can be bleak and barren. And lately the Indians have provided lots of trouble. But with your tenacity, you'd survive. However, the drive's not your biggest problem. Whittley's a more formidable obstacle."

"I thought you said he wasn't the hide-in-the-alley kind."

"He isn't . . . at least, I don't believe so. But it so happens that he's the principal owner of the Three Forks Stockyard. Most all cattle pushed through here fall under his dominion. He's the one you buy from, so he sets the price. Under the circumstances, that might be awkward."

"How about local cattlemen? Couldn't I buy from them?"

"No doubt you could. However, local beef's much more valuable than those Texas steers. Your margin of profit's cut. I suggest you and

Mudd ride out on the range to meet the incoming herds. They might sell you a few hundred head before they reach Three Forks. It's worth pursuing."

"And Mowrey can stay with us while you're gone," Melissa offered.

After dinner Bob Roy pulled on his hat, and reached for the door. "Come on, Sandy, let's take a walk."

They strolled the busy, noisy streets of Three Forks. "What about Mowrey, Sandy? What will the two of you do now?"

"I wish I knew. I'm thinking of taking her back to the Nez Percé, but I'm not sure she'd fit in there. I have a hard time talking to her. She's anxious to get married." Sandy stopped in front of a place called The Crystal Palace to button up his leather vest.

"Well, good grief, man, you are a candidate for marriage. Twenty-eight's not a kid anymore."

"Bob Roy, even if I wanted to marry her, now's not the time. Look at me—a drifter trying to find what to do, where to go, what to be. It's an impossible situation."

"Ahhh," the sheriff pointed his finger at Sandy's chest. "An impossible situation . . . just the kind to challenge a man like Sandy Thompson."

The next morning Sandy scoured the streets for Montana Mudd. He found Mudd asleep at a back table at The Yellow Pagoda Café. The proprietor had failed to rouse or move Mudd, so he was delighted to see Sandy.

Mudd kept his word about the bath, Sandy noted. In fact, Sandy almost didn't recognize him. He helped him to his horse, then they rode east out of town in the general direction of Bozeman. By early afternoon they stumbled onto a herd, a couple thousand head of Mexican beef ramrodded by a man named Clinton out of Brownsville, Texas. The entire herd, including strays, was contracted to an Indian agency in northern Montana.

"But there's another herd a day or so behind us. Don't know if they're going for Bozeman or Three Forks, though," Clinton told them. "If you want to talk to their boss, you'd better ride the gap. If they're going east, they'll leave the main trail there."

Sandy and Mudd rode hard through the long grass and rounded the hills of southern Montana. By dark they reached the Yellowstone. As they sat around the fire they wondered if this journey was worth it. "We're gonna wind up in Injun territory," Mudd warned.

"Let's just ride until noon tomorrow. If we don't see any herds, we'll turn around," Sandy suggested.

As they broke camp the next morning, Mudd questioned Sandy. "Say, do you know anything about buying Texas steers?"

"Me? This was all your plan. I assumed you were the expert."

"Yeah, the plan was mine, but I never said nothin' 'bout knowin' Texas steers. Oh, well, it shouldn't be no problem."

As they rode on, Sandy almost hoped they missed the herds after all. But just before noon they spotted them. They stalled and let them catch up.

Mudd guessed right about where the cook would set up camp for the crew. An old codger soon pulled up into the cottonwood grove. He invited them to stay for supper, and they quickly agreed. By the time the foreman and two shifts of men arrived, Sandy and Mudd pitched in finding wood and chips, and corralled horses with the wrangler.

The trail boss informed them that their drive began four months earlier at the Rio Grande. Except for a few renegade Indians, the trip ran routine, but they lost a man crossing the North Platte. "We started with twenty-four hundred eighty head. Now we've got over twenty-eight hundred. We picked them up coming across north Texas—wild stuff that'd been wandering the hills since before the war. The owner's in Three Forks right about now. He'll be looking for someone to buy the extras."

After a dinner that included the best peach dumplings Sandy ever ate, they told stories around the fire. Mudd entertained in high style, keeping the crew in stitches with one wild tale after another.

Later a young hand named Crawford pulled Sandy aside. "I left Georgia in '66. Been out here ever since. Lost my family and vision in my right eye 'cause of the war. But I still say we could have whipped them. A man come through here about a year and a half ago . . . said he'd been in Montgomery. Word was General Cooper sailed to France to round up troops to continue the fight. That so?"

"No truth to it I know of. Besides, there's not much left worth saving. The mills are destroyed, the farms in ruin, the factories shut down. The stinking carpetbaggers run things everywhere. Most of the fighting men, like you and me, we're out here. We fought a good fight. We thought the states should decide for themselves. But the country said different. Time will tell who's right."

When they bedded down close to midnight, clouds rolled in. Sandy expected a storm by morning. Within an hour lightning cracked along the eastern canyons. The foreman shouted, "All hands and the cook! Stampede!"

Sandy jumped to his feet.

The cattle ran wild as Sandy rushed to the remuda, pulling on his boots and dragging his saddle. The young Crawford insisted he take a fresh cow pony. Then, the chase began.

In their panic the cattle aimed straight for red

canyon country. If they weren't halted before they reached the canyons, the jagged lava rock and deep ravines could destroy most the herd. Sandy realized this situation called for every man.

Crawford's big black mare ran as if she would never slow down. Ghost shadows flew around them. Rocks and dry gullies leaped before them. But the mare pushed on as though this was home to her.

Riders flanked the herd on both sides, trying to keep them from spreading. Several of the men on faster mounts pushed toward the lead. Someone had to cut them off at the front. Sandy could see the trail boss riding hard up the point on the far side of the herd. He swung his arm at Sandy, motioning the direction he was going to turn them. Sandy realized his own danger. *If this horse stumbles once, I'm a dead man.*

He raked the big mare and applied the quirt as hard as he could. He attempted to ride wide to the top and catch the herd as the trail boss turned them. That way he could help circle them, and also avoid personal jeopardy.

Lightning flashed again, frenzying the beasts more. The boss's horse spooked. He reared his head, leaped high, twisted, then crashed down and stumbled, rolling momentarily. The boss was pinned, then flung free. Sensing freedom to that side, the cattle broke through. The man scrambled to his feet and dashed a hair ahead of the longhorns. The swing rider behind him couldn't overtake them.

Sandy raked the mare again and pushed her right into the fleeing cattle. One horn caught the mare's flank and ripped through Sandy's boot and pants. Yet the mare kept riding and cleared the other side of the point. Sandy forced her to the lead and cut the herd left. The swing riders teamed by forcing the cattle to circle, and kept them milling. The stampede leaders were thrown back into the drags, gradually slowing down.

A full hour later the hands relaxed their grips, but no one left the saddle. A downpour kept the herd agitated. The boss rode up on the back of Crawford's saddle. He managed a weak smile. "Don't believe I've introduced myself. The name's Jib Taylor. You want to ride? We'll sign you on any day, month, or year, y'hear? Take Crawford's slicker. We've got to ride back for new mounts."

They never left the saddles all night. A hand named Sonny relieved Sandy about daybreak to go in for chuck. The men who were there either ate their breakfast in silence or slept where they sat. Sandy's leg had stopped bleeding, so he examined the torn boot. "Good thing there's no contract doctors here," Sandy kidded with the cook. "During the war those docs worked by commission. You know, three dollars for dressing a wound, eight dollars for removing a bullet, fifty dollars for amputation. A scratch like this would be good cause for cutting off a leg. Now the East is full of unnecessary cripples."

"No need to worry," the cook answered. "We don't cut them off out here until we see the gangrene—which is usually two days too late."

Jib Taylor rode up looking as worn as the others. "We lost a couple hundred head up the dry creekbed. We're rounding them up now. Other than that, I think our main loss was a night's sleep, and about forty years off my life. When that two-bit horse balked, I thought I'd ridden my last trail. Thompson, that was a great piece of riding."

"I was probably too dumb to realize what a fool chance I took," Sandy said, embarrassed. "Did this set you back a day?"

"Actually, we might make it to Three Forks a day earlier. I just rode to the top of the ridge. If we ease this gang over the hill, we'll be ten miles closer than yesterday." He pulled out a piece of paper. "Thompson, here's a note I wrote to Don Harris. He owns the herd. I told him I think you should be able to buy the excess. But I can't guarantee he hasn't sold them already."

Mudd, who also spent the night riding, proposed they sleep until noon, then head back to town. But Sandy feared the cattle would be sold. He left Mudd with the cook and rode northwest. At midnight he lifted himself off the panting horse in front of Bob Roy's house and banged on the door.

Bob Roy welcomed him in, followed by Melissa and Mowrey, both wrapped in yellow nightrobes. Before he collapsed on the living room floor, he mumbled something about telling them all about it in the morning.

When he awoke, the sun beat hot into the Wiley home. He rushed into the kitchen where Bob Roy, Melissa, and Mowrey were eating. "I'm sorry, everyone, but I don't have time for breakfast now, I've—"

"Breakfast?" Bob Roy interrupted. "It's past noon. You'd better sit down and—"

"Noon! I've got to see a man named Harris." Sandy searched around for his hat.

"Sandy Thompson, no man on either side of the Mississippi has ever refused to sit down and eat my dumplings. And you aren't going to be the first!" Melissa firmly led him to a chair. "And besides, we have some great news for you."

Sandy attempted to hurry through the meal while Melissa talked. "When you left, Bob Roy and I tried to figure out what you should do about Mowrey, just like you asked. Well, I thought of a perfect solution, and Bob Roy agrees."

Sandy's forked paused in midair. A knot developed in his stomach.

"You and Mowrey should get married," Melissa exclaimed as though it were the first time ever mentioned. "Oh, and Mowrey said it would be all right with her."

"Bob Roy, I told you clear I wasn't looking to get married. What do you mean, letting these women carry on like this. Melissa, I don't even have a job."

"You've got capital, and a dream."

"I'm not settled down."

"Mowrey's never been settled down in her life," Melissa countered. "And Mowrey loves you. Do you love her?"

"Love! I've got to purchase cattle, and you're cramming me with dumplings and talking about love?"

Melissa didn't relent. "Answer my question, Theodore A. Thompson."

Sandy sighed. "Sure, I suppose, if pressed, I— wait! Give me a chance to think about this."

"Preacher's coming through Wednesday next," Melissa announced. "We've bought the dress. Shall we rent the hall?"

"Bob Roy, I hold you personally accountable for this. You could have prevented—"

"Now, relax, Sandy. It all makes good sense."

"Good sense! We're nothing alike!" Sandy retorted.

"You've always been a different breed yourself, Sandy," Bob Roy answered calmly.

"But, she's so young. I'm at least ten years older!" Sandy grabbed at straws as he felt the noose pull tighter.

Bob Roy stood up and held his arm out. "Hold

it, ladies. The man's got a point. That nullifies the whole works. Sandy here's too old to try to handle someone as pretty and active as Mowrey. At his age he could have a heart attack. Probably wouldn't make it through one year—"

"That does it! Rent the hall!" He turned to Mowrey. "I hope you're prepared for this because I don't know what we're getting into." As he slammed down his hat, he asked, "Do you know where I can find Don Harris?"

"He was eating lunch at The Yellow Pagoda when I came in," Bob Roy replied. "But you might want to wait until he's through. George Whittley sat with him."

"Whittley?" moaned Sandy. "He'll buy my cattle!"

Halfway across town it hit him. *How in the world did I let them talk me into agreeing to get married?* His head pounded as he tried to straighten his swirl of thoughts. *I'll just have to find a way to convince her why it won't work.* In the meantime he had Harris to find . . . and Whittley.

Thompson found them at a back table. The sight of Whittley made him think twice. Maybe he should wait until Harris left. But that was a risk, too. He finally marched up to the gray-haired man and completely ignored Whittley. "Excuse me, are you Don Harris?"

The man nodded, and Whittley rose in rage, "How dare you—"

Sandy dove right in. "I have a note here, Mr. Harris, from your trail boss." He handed Jib's letter over and kept talking. "I'd like to purchase four hundred head of your cattle. I'll be glad to take everything over your contract and drive them across to the Owyhees."

"Harris! This despicable drifter could not—"

Harris brushed him aside. "I know, George, I read the newspaper. Well, Thompson, I was just negotiating with Whittley about those same head. But if Jib Taylor says you're all right, it's good enough for me. Whittley's bid ten dollars a head, and you?"

"I'll go eleven dollars." Sandy quickly tried to figure profit and loss margin.

"Twelve dollars!" Whittley bellowed.

"Well, Mr. Harris, I guess I could go thirteen dollars . . . if me and your trail boss could cut them out."

"Sixteen dollars a head, and you cut them out," Whittley retorted.

"Harris, I really wanted those steers, but I can't compete with Whittley," Sandy resigned.

George Whittley gloated as Sandy turned on his heel. At that moment the door swung open and Jib Taylor entered. "Hey, Thompson, did you make a deal?"

"No, Mr. Whittley here outbid me." Sandy's mind raced to figure another alternative.

"Mr. Harris, could I talk to you in private?" Jib

interjected. "The herd's on the flats outside town with the men chomping to get loose."

While Taylor and Harris huddled, Sandy and Whittley continued to ignore each other. Soon, Harris walked back to them. "Whittley, I'm sorry, but I've decided to sell the excess to Thompson for thirteen dollars a head. Seems he turned a stampede around and saved Jib's life. Figure I owe him something. But I'll be glad to bring you up some extras next summer."

"But . . . but, you can't do that!" Whittley sputtered.

"I just did," Harris said.

"I warn you, if you sell to this gunslinger, I won't rent the corrals to you."

"If you don't rent me the corrals, I'll run all twenty-eight hundred head right down Main Street. Yours will be the first pulverized building." Harris stuck out a hand to Sandy. "A deal?"

Whittley stormed out of the café and Sandy discussed the details. Harris would take half the payment now and half when they returned from Silver City.

"I've been thinking of running two herds up here next year. You get to wanting some spring work, let me know. If you're interested, I'd put you and Jib on the trail by the first of April. It's hard work, and tough on a family. You got family, Thompson?"

"No . . . I mean, I might be getting married next

week." He managed to spew out the unfamiliar words.

"Well, send me a letter this winter if you're coming with me."

Sandy recalled the wedding plans again when he passed a store window displaying women's hats. He rehearsed a showdown with Mowrey.

After supper he and Mowrey sat out on the Wileys' porch. Mowrey got right to the point. "You don't want to marry me, do you?"

Sandy took a deep breath. "The whole thing's crazy. You're a beautiful young lady. But I'm new in this country, and you were born and raised in this land. And I don't know the first thing about taking care of a woman, let alone a. . . . Mowrey, the timing's off for me. I keep saying that, and no one listens. Sure, I want a place of my own someday . . . some acreage way out in the wilderness, a cozy house, a big barn, freedom to ride all day and never run into anybody, or worry about who's waiting for me in town. It's a matter of timing."

"I know, Thompson. I know about the mill money back in Virginia. I know about Grandview. I know about your sister, and the war. But don't you see that you and me have a lot in common? We both have our past, but neither of us has a future. Why couldn't we find one together? I won't slow you down. I can ride, I can rope, I can shoot."

Sandy couldn't think of anything to say.

"I want to look at your sunsets. And I'd very much like you to look at mine. I don't know if that's what getting married means for sure, but it sounds good to me. I don't want to be alone. You've been alone a long time, and I can see what it's done to you."

"But it's just not done this way, not where I come from. We need to get to know each other, get acquainted with kinfolk, talk to a minister, really think it through."

"But neither of us has any real family, and I know I like being near you very much. I know you're a fair man . . . a strong, yet gentle man. I know I could be very proud to tell others that you were my husband. Most of all, you're a man who keeps his word. If you told me you'd take care of me, I know you would."

Sandy leaned against the porch steps. "This is such a wild, uncertain land . . . ," he began vaguely.

"This is my land, and I believe, Thompson, it's your land as well."

"But, marriage is such a big commitment. . . ."

"Today you dove right into the cattle business. You don't know much about that, either. Do you always know everything about a venture before you try it?"

"You sound like a Boston lawyer."

"And you sound like a superstitious Indian grandmother. Thompson, I'm got going to plead with you, and I will not complain any more about your decision. But my father always said we must do those things in life we'd regret not doing." Her voice lowered, and she raised her eyes to his only on the last few words. "And I would regret not telling you that I want to marry you."

Mowrey's words began to penetrate. He even thought he began to understand. Moments like this of sharing had been missing from his life for ten long years. After a long silence he said, "Mowrey, I can't promise you much."

"But you'll take care of me?" she said softly.

"That's about it." He looked into her deep, dark eyes.

"And I'll take care of you," she whispered. "That's enough for now." She kissed him gently on the cheek, and for what seemed an eternity Sandy Thompson and Mowrey, two orphans, clung tightly to each other.

Sandy shivered in the sudden brisk winds as Mowrey slipped inside the house. He slowly rose from the porch and heaved a deep sigh. His life had not simplified, but for the moment it just didn't matter.

While Mowrey and Melissa prepared for the wedding, Sandy and Mudd pulled their gear together for the trip to the Owyhee Mountains. They decided to take three horses apiece in the remuda, so they purchased some fron Don Harris. Sandy made sure the black mare was among them. They also bought twelve additional horses to sell in the gold country as well.

At one time, Harris expressed concern. "I don't think just the two of you can push those head clear across the territory. You'll need help. Maybe a couple of my men will sign on."

Mudd roared. "If any are fool enough, send them over." None came.

On Monday, Bob Roy brought home a young boy he had chased out of the bakery. "Says he's a trail hand and needs a job. Think you could use him?"

"Did you ever ride for Jib Taylor?" Sandy asked.

"Yeah, last year. But I wintered here trying to find some gold," the black-haired boy claimed.

"How old are you?"

The youth looked down at his boots. "Sixteen years and two days."

Bob Roy invited him to stay for dinner, and Clay Kelly was hired on for the drive.

Sandy tried to pull the details together. Wednesday they'd get married. Friday they'd start on the drive, with Mowrey staying with Melissa until they returned.

Mowrey had other thoughts. "Thompson, I'm not marrying you so I can sit at Three Forks while you have all the fun."

"But this trek's dangerous for any man. Don Harris said so."

"No, what we both agreed was that we'd share

sunsets. That means being together. You can still leave Thursday, but I'm going, too."

"But, we don't have supplies for you."

"I have my own supplies, thank you. And you'll need someone to cook and wrangle the horses. You'll all die from your own cooking."

For the first time Sandy noticed a slight tilt of Mowrey's nose. He had the sudden feeling there was a lot about Mowrey he hadn't noticed before. "OK, you can go. But if we're going to be married, can't you call me something besides Thompson?"

"You call me Mowrey, so I call you Thompson."

Bob Roy's suit hung loose on Sandy, but the tie felt like it would cut off all circulation as he paced in front of the mirror. He stiffened his back and tried to stroll casually into Melissa's decorated hall. Piles of food filled tables along one wall. The room filled with townspeople, most not acquainted with Sandy and Mowrey. Melissa explained that weddings in Three Forks drew folks from the whole area.

Sandy looked the crowd over. Mudd and their new hired man, Clay Kelly, sat in the front row. Harris, Taylor, and a few cowhands stood at the rear. The editor of the *Examiner* held pencil and paper in hand. A stout lady pumped away on the organ as Mowrey appeared at the end of the aisle. She reached out her arm to Sandy. Her olive skin and raven hair swept up behind dramatically accented her white lace dress. She looked like a fairytale princess. For Sandy, the ceremony took on the aura of a dream.

They walked down the aisle while everyone rose to their feet. Bob Roy and Melissa greeted them at the front as their attendants. The preacher stepped forward. Sandy's chest throbbed.

"Dearly beloved—"

Mowrey startled everyone, including the preacher, by interrupting. "Mr. Thompson," she said, loud enough for everyone to hear, "are you a Christian?"

"What?"

"Are you a Christian?" she repeated distinctly.

"Mowrey, this is no time to discuss religion. We can talk about it later." Sandy sensed the audience straining to catch every detail.

"I want to know if you're a Christian. I told my mother I wouldn't marry a pagan."

"A pagan!"

"Yes. I can't marry a pagan. I've been a pro-fessing Christian since I was seven years old."

Sandy heard chuckles behind him. "Of course I'm a Christian!" Sandy said through his gritted teeth. "Now let's get on with it."

"It takes more than talk," she continued.

"Mowrey—!"

"You have to have a personal commitment," she said, more earnest than ever.

Bob Roy broke in. "Mowrey, I know Sandy's a Christian. I was there when he was baptized in the river. I saw him go clear under!"

"Good." She smiled. "Let's go ahead then."

The preacher cleared his throat. "We are assembled here in the presence of God to join—"

Mowrey turned to Sandy again. "Does this mean you're a Baptist?"

Sandy pulled out a handkerchief and wiped his forehead. "Yes, yes! Is that all right?"

"But, I'm a Presbyterian. My name's on the roll at the mission at Lapwai—"

The preacher tried to cut her off. "And you, er, Mowrey, do you take Theodore Arthur Thompson to be your wedded husband, and do you promise to . . ."

"Melissa," Mowrey blurted out, "can a Baptist marry a Presbyterian?"

". . . in plenty and in want . . ."

"I certainly hope so, honey. I'm a strict Episcopalian, and Bob Roy's Baptist."

". . . as long as you both shall live?"

Everyone in the hall stared at Mowrey. "Oh, yes—I do, I really do!"

The laughter and applause served as background music for the rest of the ceremony. Within a few moments, Sandy Thompson had become a husband, and Mowrey had become a wife.

An hour later they found themselves alone at the

punch bowl. "Mowrey, why all the fuss down at the altar?"

"I had to. Seeing the preacher and hearing the music, I remembered everything I'd been taught, and I'd been afraid to say anything before."

"Why?"

"I wanted to marry you so much, I was afraid of what you'd say. But still, it's very important to me. So, I waited as long as I could to find out."

"Mowrey, God's important to me, too. It's just that my life's been out of control so long. A man tends to push some things aside . . . like the faith of his childhood." He stepped closer and cradled her gently in his arms. "But now that I've got one of the prettiest of God's creations for my wife. . . ." He put his lips close to her ear. "I really do love you, Mowrey."

Her eyes glistened as he added, "And I don't think anyone would notice if we just disappeared."

The honeymoon suite at Three Forks' finest hotel didn't compare to Eastern standards, but Sandy hardly noticed. The newlyweds appeared downstairs the next morning at eleven. Mudd greeted them in the lobby. "The kid's holding the herd on the flats south of town. You want us to make camp for the night, or are we really leaving today?"

By three in the afternoon, 431 cattle, a dozen horses, six pack mules carrying chuck, and four riders rode south out of Montana Territory. At sunset they set up their first camp. Sandy stayed with the cattle while the others ate. Clay Kelly relieved him right before dark.

"Mudd, is that yours?" Sandy pointed at the small white tent pitched next to the trees.

"Ain't mine," the old man said, grinning through his gold and gaping teeth.

"I put it up," Mowrey announced, as she filled a dish for Sandy.

"It's too small for all of us," Sandy noted.

"It's not set up for *all* of us," Mowrey replied with indignance.

"But we've been together over a month sleeping out in the open. Why a tent?"

"Because then I was just Mowrey, the Indian girl."

"And now?"

"Now, I am Mrs. Thompson."

CHAPTER
11

A routine of traveling without directions, riding in the dust of the herd, eating on the run, sleeping on the ground, and changing night duty every three hours quickly fell into place by the third day. The crew followed the Jefferson southeast of Three Forks—an easy ride, with plenty of grass for the cattle. Day by day they paralleled the Jefferson, then the Beaverhead, and finally the Red Rock, just east of Bannock.

Along the way they learned something about driving cattle. Clay Kelly proved to be the teacher. Clay rode point while Sandy and Mudd covered the swings, keeping the herd from getting too wide. Mowrey packed camp and pushed the drags along until she needed to pass the herd to set up ahead for the next meal.

In the evenings, Sandy doubled the night watch when there were signs of a storm. The bout with the stampede had alerted him. By the time they reached the Continental Divide at Monida Pass, the saddle-broken team knew most of the cows by sight. An old red-faced cow seemed to give them the most trouble. Sandy determined to butcher her first, should they get that hungry.

But their food supply abounded. Mudd brought down a buffalo. Sandy shot several antelope. Once they crossed the Divide into Idaho, however, the game thinned. So did the grass and water and trail.

Two weeks later they saw their first humans. While Mowrey set up camp near Camas Creek, three men approached. She was alone with a pack string and nine horses.

"Where'd you steal those horses, squaw?" the leader snarled, keeping a roving eye on the surrounding country.

Mowrey continued preparation of the meal. "I didn't steal them."

"Of course you stole them. They've got white man's shoes on them. Sure aren't Indian horses. Look like cow ponies off the Double B. Say, didn't you boys hear Stephens says he's missing some stock?"

"You're right, Tommy. I think they do look like Double B animals. What's the matter, did your old man run off to the hills when he saw us a-comin'?"

Mowrey picked up a large hunting knife. "My husband and his men will ride over that hill any moment. If any of his property's touched, you can be assured the sun won't rise until the matter's settled."

"Hey, a feisty one. Nothing more fun than a feisty squaw. I say we tie her up and take her with us," the leader said.

Mowrey kept doing busy work around the camp, with knife in hand, while easing toward a pack mule which carried a loaded revolver. The three men, still mounted, mumbled among themselves. Then they dismounted and spread out, circling Mowrey from all sides. She seemed oblivious to them as she yanked cast-iron pans from the pack.

"Now, there's no need to be afraid. You just come along and find out what real men are like," one taunted.

Mowrey tossed down a skillet that clanged and

bounced off a rock. Her right hand pointed a loaded .44. "Before you come a step closer, I want you real men to decide which one of you will be buried right here in your tracks. If any of you goes for a gun, I'm pulling the trigger. Which one of you real men wants to be the first?"

They stopped their pacing. "Shoot, there ain't no greasy squaw that's worth a big fuss. Let's get the horses and go," said the eldest of the three, turning toward the remuda. Mowrey cocked the pistol, and he froze in place. "That's not a very smart thing to do, squaw. You see, if you don't let us ride out of here with those horses, all we have to do is wait until dark to shoot you and take everything."

"Provided I don't shoot you all right now," Mowrey replied.

"We'll be back, and you'll be sorry you weren't more hospitable," he growled as they sped off south.

Before their dust settled, Sandy rode up. "Saw some riders. We having company for dinner?"

"No, they aren't staying," Mowrey said, still holding the .44.

"Not hungry, huh?" Sandy prodded with a grin.

"They wanted more than we could give," Mowrey reported, and returned to her chores.

The next several days Mowrey watched for the men's return. The third morning, just before noon, riders appeared out of the east. She grabbed a Winchester and hid behind some rocks. This time

Sandy and the crew rode near enough to come running at the sound of a shot. She aimed the rifle at the lead rider.

The bright sun caused their hats to cast dark shadows across their faces, but as they drew nearer she recognized the leader and lowered her weapon.

"You doin' some huntin', Mowrey?" greeted Pop Bradley.

"This is bushwhacker country, you know," she explained with a smile. "What brings you trappers this far out of the hills?"

"We heard there was a weddin' in town, and since we didn't get an invite, we decided to come down and invite ourselves to dinner." Branch, Pop, Wayne Jared, and a couple of other men from the rendezvous dismounted and pulled off their saddles. "I hear you're headin' for the Owyhees—"

A piercing Rocky Mountain yell halted Pop's remarks. Montana Mudd swooped down the hill at the sight of his old gang. Sandy galloped close behind. Mudd leapt from his mount and danced a jig with Pop Bradley. "It's been awhile since I seen regular folks," Mudd roared.

Branch shook Sandy's hand. "We come for the weddin' reception. Me and the boys were sorry to miss the doin's in Three Forks, so we brought you this." Branch pulled out a wooden box from his saddlebag. He presented it to Mowrey, who carefully slid open the lid. She opened the drawstring of a red felt sack and pulled out a shiny silver and gold clock.

"Doesn't exactly fit the trail," said Wayne Jared with a wink, "but when you and Thompson set up house, it'll look real handsome. Something to remind him what time he should be home nights." The men all beamed with awkward pleasure at their offering.

Mowrey traced the detailed craftmanship with her finger, then cradled it in Sandy's hands. "Fellas, you sort of went overboard. I mean, this is one beautiful timepiece," Sandy gently scolded.

Pop Bradley explained. "Well, we figured you're a money-makin' man for us. Most of us won some bettin' on you against the brave. Then we got forty dollars apiece when we ran into Grandview. So we're just paying your commission, you might say."

"A commission with interest, I'd say." Sandy admired the clock a moment longer, then handed it back to Mowrey. "By the way, what did you do with Grandview?"

"Well, Jared came off with the best idea," Branch said as they all plopped down in the shade. "He suggested we fill Grandview full of rotgut, then lock him in an empty whiskey barrel and ship him off to St. Louis."

Sandy and Mudd whooped with delight. "Then

what?" Sandy asked, as he kicked off a boot and dumped out some sand.

"We didn't quite make it. We got him passed out on the whiskey, but for the life of us we couldn't shove him down one of those barrels. So we rode into Bozeman, nailed him into a packing crate, and put him on a stage to St. Louis. When we hit Three Forks last week, we ran across Louie LaFever, fresh from Cheyenne. He saw Grandview there hiring guns to ride with him. He couldn't tell if Grandview was coming after us or after you. Thought you oughta know."

"We shoulda shot the rattlesnake," Pop offered.

"I'm sorry to have you men tangled up in my mess," Sandy said.

Pop snorted. "They could send the whole army into these mountains and not bother us. It's you we're concerned about."

"Thanks, but we should be pretty safe now. Only a fool'd follow us on this path to Silver City."

"Well, it seems to us Grandview ain't noted for his brains," Branch stated, and they all nodded in agreement.

Sandy tried to pass it off. "By tomorrow we'll be in sight of the Snake. From then on it'll be pretty hard for anyone to sneak up on us. By now Grandview's probably chasing somebody else."

That night everybody danced to Pop's harmonica. They took turns spinning Mowrey, but most times they didn't bother with a partner. The hunters took shifts with the herd, so all could enjoy the party. When morning broke, the camp looked like a massacre, with bodies spread everywhere. The only ones who stirred were Mowrey and Sandy. Mowrey boiled coffee, and Sandy tended the herd. When Clay Kelly took over, he returned to find Branch and the others saddling up.

"Sure appreciate the warning," Sandy told them. "And it's always good to have company on the trail."

Pop Bradley was the last of the string to leave. "You get in serious trouble, just head for the hills. We'll be up there somewhere. You can count on us for help."

With the desert ahead, the trail south grew bleaker. Some Indians appeared on the southern horizon one day, but didn't approach any closer. Each morning the herd and men left camp early to get moving before the heat got to them. Mowrey cleaned camp, loaded the pack mules, and rounded up horses. One day she had just mounted her Appaloosa gelding when six men rode up. She expected trouble, so she grabbed for the stock of her Winchester. But suddenly the strong arm of a seventh rider grabbed her wrist.

"So, we meet again." It was the same man who had accosted her earlier. "I came for my horses." He jerked her off the horse and sent her tumbling to the ground. She tried to race for the rocks to the south in hopes of attracting Sandy. One of the men galloped hard toward her, while the others rounded the horses and pack animals. As the man closed in on Mowrey and stretched to pick her up, he got a surprise. Instead of struggling to get away, she jumped up, grabbed tight to his arm, then used all her weight to unbalance him. He was thrown off his horse right on top of her.

She slammed her knee hard into his groin, then kicked him in the head. When she ran for the rocks again, another man followed her, but then stopped after a few yards. "This is lava rock," he yelled. "I can't ride a pony through there. It'd cut his feet to shreds."

The men headed north with their bounty as Mowrey skimmed through the rocks and out to the prairie. When she finally spotted the herd in the distance she kept running hard as she could. Clay Kelly saw her and fired a warning shot to the others. Mudd and Sandy sped over. "The men from the other day returned . . . took the remuda and chuck . . . gone north," she panted.

Sandy held her shoulders and looked into her eyes. "Are you all right?"

"Yes, but we must hurry. If they find a canyon or hit timber, we'll lose them."

"How many of them?" Sandy began checking the ammunition in his Winchester.

"Seven . . . at least that was all I counted."

"Clay, I hope you can use that gun you carry."

"I'll do you proud, boss, but what about the herd?"

"Mowrey, you stay—" Sandy barely got the words out.

"Mr. Thompson, I'm going with you. Those bullies have pushed me for the last time. Besides, I'm a better shot than Mudd, since he won't shoot anything anyway."

Mudd didn't protest being left behind. But three against seven didn't sound too encouraging. It wouldn't take long to get the riders in sight, but how would they catch them unawares? It was too early in the day to wait until dark.

Sandy sighted a jagged canyon cutting into the prairie. He led the others slowly down to its bottom. "I think this is the same canyon that circles around to meet the trail at the cottonwood trees. We just might have a chance, but if they catch us down here, we're sitting ducks."

The horses proved their worth by riding the rocks well. In little more than an hour they reached the far end, close to the cottonwoods. They could see the riders approaching fast from the south. Sandy gave orders. "Clay and I will take separate sides of the trees. Mowrey, you wait at the canyon mouth."

But before Sandy could stop her, Mowrey clutched her rifle and scaled one of the tallest trees. Sandy and Clay squeezed into place just as the lead rider came into view.

The men dismounted as they entered the grove.

When the leader of the group walked under Mowrey's tree, she leapt down on him and drove the butt of her rifle into the back of his head. A warning shot from Sandy froze the others in place. When one man tried to draw, he caught the lead from Clay Kelly's Colt. Sandy shouted at the five remaining, "Drop the guns, quick!"

One of them hesitated. Lead hit the dust just a foot in front of him. He threw down his weapon. Sandy marched them together and sat them down. "Horse stealing's a hanging offense. But I don't have enough rope for all of you, so if you'd just tell me who's responsible."

A red-faced kid answered. "It was East . . . Tommy East . . . over there, under the squaw. He said these were Double B horses and we'd get a reward for bringing them back from the Indians. I ain't no horse thief, mister. We thought these had been stolen by Indians." The other men blurted out agreement.

"Mowrey, which of these men did you see the other day?" Sandy inquired.

"This one, the one he called East, and the one Clay shot . . . and the fellow in the gray shirt."

"OK, the rest of you leave your guns and boots right here and ride north fast."

"Our boots?" the red-faced one complained.

"You heard right." Clay cleared their saddles of weapons, and the four mounted barefoot and rode away.

The gray-shirted one began to plead. "Hey, let us go, mister. Rainy here's hurt bad. Besides, you got your stock back. Ain't no harm except one scared squaw."

Sandy raised his rifle and cocked the trigger at the insult.

"My God, man, no!" the man cried, with his arms flung over his face.

"Wait, Thompson," Mowrey shouted. "Toss me a knife. I think this one's coming to."

As East's eyes opened in a glaze, Mowrey jerked his head back by the hair. She rested the cold steel of Sandy's blade against his throat. "Just how low should I draw the knife?"

East froze in fear.

Clay then spooked the riders' three horses away.

"You aren't taking our horses?" the gray-shirted one sputtered.

"I wouldn't take a man's horse," Sandy retorted. "They'll be scattered down in the canyon. You should catch them in a day or two."

"Provided Indians don't find them first," Clay added.

They sighted Fort Hall the third day after the horse-thief incident. By nightfall they bedded the cattle down just across from the fort. The next morning they planned to push the cattle across the Snake River. "The snows must have been awful heavy in those Tetons," Clay Kelly reported. "The Snake's full to the brim."

The Fort Hall crossing was well used and shallow, but Kelly knew that the swift current could bog the cattle. He suggested constructing a raft to ferry Mowrey and the supplies across first.

They quickly built a strong raft, using the trees washed up on the river's edge from the spring floods. Then the three men watched from the shore as Mowrey paddled downstream, then across. They moved the herd upstream before they charged them into the water. Clay borrowed Sandy's black mare to push the remuda across. He returned soaking wet, but with a big grin. "I could tell she was a fine swimmer," he said.

For the cattle, Sandy and Clay decided to ride point, pushing the first few head into the water. Mudd would bring up the drags.

"We got to work hard at gettin' those first few movin'," Clay instructed. "Once the others see them enter the water, they'll follow. If these long-horns walked all the way from Texas, it's not the first river they've crossed."

Sandy and Clay maneuvered the lead steer about a hundred feet from the bank, then charged them. Sandy splashed in water up to his knees before he realized the cattle were not moving. They refused to do more than drink the water. Two more tries didn't convince them. Even Clay's gunfire failed to motivate them.

"They just ain't swimmers," Mudd hollered, as he rode up. "Some folks is the same way, too . . . just ain't swimmers."

"Well, there's no way to get to Silver City without crossing that river. They've got to get across." Sandy felt his irritation rising.

"Maybe we could raft them," Mudd proposed.

"That sounds like an all-winter job," Sandy groaned. "We couldn't carry more than a few head at a time, if we'd get them on at all. Then the raft would be a mile downstream."

About then, the big red cow that always hassled them, trotted down the riverbed, breaking herd and bellowing.

"She lost that sickly calf of hers. Maybe it wandered that direction," Clay called out.

He was right. In a few minutes Sandy returned with cow and calf, and an idea. "I'm riding out in the middle of the river with the calf in my lap. It should raise quite a holler. Clay, you keep the mother roped at the back of the leaders. When I signal, you turn her loose, then shove the others toward the bank again."

Clay dropped a line around the red cow. Sandy scooped up the kicking, screaming calf. He was glad it wasn't too healthy. It was all he could do to ride bareback and hold it. Sandy's mare swam right out into midstream as Sandy managed to wave his hat at Clay. He cut the mother loose and pushed the leaders to the river again.

The big red cow barged into the river, bellowing the whole way. Sandy kept the noisy calf well ahead of her as she swam after it. The leaders pursued behind. They swam as though it were second nature, their earlier balks forgotten. Even the drags made it.

Sandy headed back across the water to help with the strays, then spied Mudd sitting on the opposite bank. He hailed him from midstream. "How come you're not following the cows? You'll be late for chuck!"

"Send the raft back," Mudd yelled.

"What?"

"Doggone it! I can't swim! And I don't aim to start learning now."

"Mudd, all you have to do is hold on. The horse'll do the swimming for you."

"Can't do it," Mudd hollered back. "The horse'll balk, or fall. Maybe he can't swim, either."

Mudd raved on, but Sandy couldn't hear him. He yelled back, "Push out into that water, Mudd!" and returned to shore where Clay and Mowrey were starting a bonfire.

The three watched Mudd rake his horse, close his eyes, and white-knuckle the mane. A few minutes later, horse and rider emerged amidst cheers on the other side. Clay helped them up the last embankment. "You can let go now, Mudd, you're over."

Clay told Sandy and Mowrey later, "He came out

of that water mumbling something about 'walking through the valley of the shadow of death.'"

"Well," Sandy laughed, "that's gotten him out of tough times before."

By evening they dried out enough to enter Fort Hall for supplies. Sandy agreed to take a sack of mail to Silver City and some extra supplies for a bogged-down wagon train.

They followed the old Oregon Trail for about a week, without any sign of the wagon train. Then, at midday, Clay saw wagon silhouettes on the horizon. He circled the herd and rode back to the others. "I think we'd better take it easy," he suggested. "Somehow it don't look right."

Sandy left Mudd and Mowrey with the herd. Clay and Sandy approached with caution. The wagons seemed to be stuck in the mud, but from a distance they couldn't see any people. "Maybe they had to leave 'em," Clay suggested.

Then, they saw the bodies.

Scattered around the wagons lay men, women, and children, arrow-ridden and mutilated. The wagons and bodies had been stripped of anything valuable.

"Should we try to bury them?" Clay whispered.

Sandy fought back rising nausea. "No, whoever did this isn't far away. We'd better keep going . . . can't do much for these poor folks anyway."

"Look!" Clay shouted, then dismounted. He ran toward the reeds along the river, startling three children hiding there. They took off running, but he chased them down and caught the youngest who shook with fright. The eldest, a girl, cried, "Ma and Pa's dead. Jimmy, Jake, and me's all that's left."

"Come on with us, honey," Sandy offered as he rode up. "We'll take you back to Fort Hall."

"Can't go," she replied. "I promised Pa I'd get us to Oregon. We got family in Oregon."

"Well, you can't stay here, and we're going close by to Oregon."

They rode the children back to the herd. After a quick meal, the three orphans drifted off into restless sleep without saying any more than their names and that they wanted to go to Redstone, Oregon.

The next day the children rode bareback. Mowrey cleaned and fed them and helped them along the trail. They began to talk a little, but did not say a word about what happened at the wagons.

They followed the Oregon Trail as far as they could before turning up to the Owyhees. On the day before the cutoff, they discovered another emigrant wagon train with over a hundred wagons. Sandy caught up with the train captain to tell him about the children they'd found. "Those folks started out with us," he informed Sandy. "But they insisted on trying a shortcut out of Fort Hall."

Several families offered to take the children to Oregon. Sandy gave them the extra supplies they'd received from Fort Hall. As they set out, Mowrey cried. *They're tough kids. They'll make it,* she thought to herself.

The trip up into the Owyhees drained them physically, but otherwise they encountered no hazards. Four days after leaving the wagon train, they herded the cattle right through Silver City, and into the city corral.

As Sandy rode through town he glimpsed the profile of a man who looked like Robert Grandview. He was walking by the bank a few blocks away. Turning in the saddle for a closer look, he saw a young boy about five years old who was sitting by a horse trough. Around his neck he wore a gold medallion, just like the one Sandy's sister, Darlene, used to wear.

CHAPTER
12

The next time Sandy observed the boy he was squatting on the outside stairway of the *Silver City Avalanche* office. The lad never looked up as Sandy walked closer to scrutinize the medallion.

"Son, that's a mighty fine necklace you're wearing," Sandy said softly.

"Belongs to my mother," the boy said flatly. He

shaded the sun from his eyes with a dirty hand. His greasy overalls and jacket fit him snugly. He wore no shoes.

"Does your mother's name happen to be Darlene?" Sandy prepared for the response.

"Nope," he said.

"Well, what is her name?" Sandy prompted, with some disappointment.

"Momma," he replied.

"Where is your momma?" Sandy continued to pry.

"She's with Jesus." The boy stared down the road as though waiting for someone.

"With Jesus?"

"Yeah, she's dead." The boy raised up and began to walk away.

"Son, would you mind if I looked at the picture inside your locket?"

The boy's eyes reflected light for the first time. "No," he said, opening it. "Here, see, it's my grandma and grandpa. They have lots of money and live on a big farm far, far away."

Sandy felt numb as he recognized the picture of his own father and mother. The last time he saw it was the day Darlene left Virginia. Was she dead now? Where was Peter McCally, her husband? He fought to keep back the tears. "Is your father around?" he said as lightly as he could.

"Sure. He'll be back soon. Gone over to the Cosmos Silver Mine." The boy looked down the street again.

"When did he leave?"

"Yesterday."

"Yesterday? You haven't seen him since *yesterday?* Where do you live? What have you eaten?" Sandy's face flushed with anger.

"I slept under these stairs. And Miss Reynolds gave me some eggs this morning. Dad'll be back anytime now."

Just then Mowrey walked up. "Thompson, I've been looking all over for you."

"Thompson? That's like my grandma and grandpa's name," the boy said, excitedly. "Their name's Thompson."

"Son, did your mother ever tell you about her brother? Did she mention you have an uncle?"

"Yes." He brightened again. "My Uncle Teddy is the best horse rider in the whole wide world."

Sandy had to turn his head to pull out his bandana and dab at his eyes. "It's the dust," he told Mowrey, then turned hack to the boy. "What's your name, son?"

"David J. McCally," he announced with pride.

"And your father's name is Peter?"

"Maybe. Do you know my daddy?"

"Listen to me, David. My name's Sandy Thompson. But my sister's the only one in the world who ever called me Teddy. Those people in your picture happen to be my mother and father, and that means I'm your Uncle Teddy!" He picked up the boy with one arm. "Do you understand?"

The boy was all smiles. "You mean my very own Uncle Teddy?"

"That's right, and this is your Aunt Mowrey."

"I don't have an Aunt Mowrey."

"You do now. And Aunt Mowrey will take you to buy a big breakfast and a hot bath. Then she'll pick out some new clothes for you . . . maybe even a pair of boots."

"I don't like wearing shoes," he said. "But I sure am hungry!"

"Hey! Hey you!" A voice from across the street startled them. "What are you doing with my kid! Put him down or I'll—"

"McCally, this boy's the only thing that prevents me from busting your head!"

Mowrey took David from him and led him to a nearby café.

"Where's that squaw taking my kid?" McCally yelled, running toward Sandy.

"She's the boy's aunt, and it's about time he had a decent meal. Now, why don't you and me step into the alley. You've got a lot of fast talking to do. What happened to Darlene?"

Peter McCally gaped. "Sandy Thompson? Is it really you? It's been so many years and so much has happened. Hey, I know this don't look good, but things have been tough. . . ."

Sandy steered the nervous man with the handlebar mustache into an alley between the *Avalanche* office and the Idaho Hotel. "Start talking," he ordered.

"Well, we were out in California until two years ago. I worked a lumber mill and Darlene took in sewing. Little David was born there. We kept trying to find a gold strike, but it seems we got to California too late. The big companies had all the gold, and the trailings wouldn't even pay wages. So, we came up here. It was just opening up and there was plenty of room.

"About six days after we crossed the mountains, we were traveling up the Humboldt when a band of Cayuse renegades came down on us. Before I could even grab a rifle I took a shot in the shoulder. It knocked me clean out of the wagon. The horses bolted and Darlene tried to grab the reins. But by then things were out of control. The wagon flipped about three times. Darlene held onto David. I lay there helpless and watched it roll.

"About then some men from a big emigrant train rode over the hill and chased off the Indians. But by the time I struggled over to the smashed wagon, Darlene was gone, but David was safe in his mother's arms." McCally stopped to brush his cheeks. Sandy didn't bother; he just let the tears flow.

"We buried her along the trail, and David and I made it up to the Owyhees. Seems I was about two years late here, too. I've been just getting by doing odd jobs."

McCally paused a moment, then lit up as

though he just remembered some good news. "But things are looking different now. I finally got a break. I've been all day and night planning with the night foreman over at the Cosmos. There's rumors that a strike's been found on the Fraser, up in Canada. We set up a partnership and we'll head up there right away. If there's half the gold they say, I'll be a wealthy man by Christmas. Sandy, why don't you come with us? You can't miss on this one."

"What about David? You going to drag him to another gold camp?"

"Why, no. We're just moving north, that's all. Besides, what choice do I have?"

"I'll give you one—leave the boy with me and my wife. After you strike it rich, come back and make a home for him. You can't raise a kid out of a grub bag."

"You're right, Sandy, you're sure right. If you and the missus don't mind. It'll only be for a few months at the most."

"Save that speech for David. You just get the boy's gear and meet us at the Idaho Hotel, so you can tell him good-bye."

McCally hemmed and hawed. "Actually, times been so hard. I mean, what the boy has on him's all he's got."

A well-fed David McCally sat proudly at the Idaho Hotel. "Uncle Teddy, did you know that Aunt Mowrey's part Nez Percé Indian?"

"I sure did, David. Say, how about you coming to live with me and Aunt Mowrey for awhile? Your daddy needs to go to Canada to work a new job."

Before the boy answered, Peter McCally strode through the door. "Hey, Dad, can I stay with Aunt Mowrey? She's going to buy me some more clothes and a horse and some boots. Do I have to wear boots?" David screwed up his face at his dad.

Sandy and Mowrey left McCally alone with his son for a few minutes. Mowrey spoke in a low tone. "Have you considered what kind of life David will have with us? We aren't settled down either."

"I'll figure it out as we go along. For now, I've got to get him off the streets. Then, I need to sell those cows. One thing at a time."

Sandy and McCally walked out on the wooden sidewalk of Washington Street. "When are you leaving?" Sandy inquired.

"Tomorrow . . . maybe even today, now that David's cared for. You got to get there early to make your claim or there's nothing left. Oh, where am I going to find you and David when I come back?"

"Check with Sheriff Bob Roy Wiley at Three Forks, Montana. He'll know where we are. After I sell some head, I'm going to return there."

"If you got cows to sell, try Amster Norris over at the Shoenbar Mill. Word has it he pays top dollar." McCally offered his hand to Sandy. "See you later in the year. And thanks."

Sandy paused, then took the hand. "Sure."

Sandy checked them all into the nicest rooms he could find at the Idaho Hotel. Silver City was definitely a cut above cow towns like Three Forks. The man at the desk studied his name. "So you're Thompson? What a shame. A friend's been in here several days asking for you. He finally decided you weren't coming and left this morning. Must have been a really good friend. Said he'd ride all the way to California to find you."

"Did he happen to leave his name?"

"I believe he said it was Grandview. Yes, that's it, Grandview."

If Grandview had actually left town this morning for California, Sandy could relax. But until he could be certain, he walked the streets with care, cutting through as many sidepaths as possible. When he couldn't find Mudd or Clay, he hiked to the Shoenbar Mill alone.

Amster Norris pored over some books behind a large oak desk. He strained to find a ten dollar error. In a large business like his, ten dollars was nothing. But Norris had gotten to where he was by being careful. Sometimes he marveled at his success. "Just a Texas cowman who chased some strays up a canyon and into a silver mine," he liked to brag. There were days when thoughts of that simple cowman's life appealed to him. He felt like a lonesome cowboy stuck in an office. This was one of those days.

Sandy's arrival intruded on this task. "Mr. Norris? I'm Sandy Thompson. I just drove four hundred thirty-one Texas longhorns from Montana, and I heard you do some cattle buying. Do you think you might be interested?"

"Thompson, I'll tell you what I'm interested in. I'd like to be out there about the North Platte with twenty-five hundred head of contract beef. Don't ever own a silver mine, Thompson. The book work drives you crazy. And the money worries you so much, you don't have any fun anymore. But, to your question. Yes, I buy beef. Let me get my hat and we'll go down to look at your stock. If they have any meat on them at all I'll give you twenty-six dollars a head for them. Not a penny more. But I'll wager that's two dollars better than anyone else in town."

They strode to the corrals, Norris talking the whole time.

Norris liked the beef and bid on the extra horses as well. The way he examined the beef and the way he sized up each horse's weaknesses and strengths, Sandy knew he dealt with a cattleman. The two developed a quick friendship.

"Tell you what, Thompson. I'll take every head you bring across the territory. Even advance you a little if you need the capital. And one of these days, let's bring a herd of these beauties all the way from the Rio Grande itself. Now, take this note down to the bank. Have Hawkins draw up a bill of sale, and collect your money. Too bad you didn't want to sell that black mare. She's a night rider and swimmer if I ever saw one."

"Mr. Norris," Sandy said with a nod, "you've made yourself a deal, and an admirer. You're a fine judge of stock. Someday I'll take you up on those other offers."

Sandy wound back through town to find Mudd and the bank. They spied each other across Washington Street and met in the middle of the thoroughfare as freight wagon trains pulled in from all directions. Mudd had been working on a deal himself.

"The best we can do is twenty-four dollars a head." Mudd spat in the dirt and kicked dust. "Several merchants told me the same story. Beef price is actually on the way down up here. Another couple years it might even get normal. Say, I did hear of a fellow named Norris, but he buys just from old cronies."

"Mudd, I just made a deal with Norris for twenty-six dollars a head. He'll take the horses, too." He threw his arm around the old trader. "Now, if you have time to go to the bank, we can carry your pay out in a sack. This means we'll each clear over three thousand dollars apiece. Can you imagine that?"

They walked out of the bank feeling like the

richest men on earth. "Let's pay Clay, then Mowrey and I are going shopping. How about you, Mudd? What are your plans for Silver City?"

His gold-toothed partner just grinned. "I've got some shopping of my own to do."

"Mudd, we promised Clay a hundred dollars for his part. But remember, he was the only one who'd come with us greenhorns, and then we figured on only twenty-five dollars a head. I say we give Clay one dollar per cow. Might be just the break the kid needs. I doubt if we could have made it in by now without him."

Mudd agreed. They found Clay at the barbershop. He was overwhelmed with the bonus. "Look, you earned every penny of it," Sandy assured him. "Now, don't chuck-a-luck it all away. It should keep you eating through the winter, providing you find a cheaper place than Silver City."

"Don't worry about me, boss. I ain't no tinhorn. And you did all right for it bein' your first drive. I'll even sign on for another run. Sandy, in my book you'll do to ride the river with."

Mudd and Thompson headed for the Idaho Hotel. "You reckon Grandview's left town?" Mudd ventured.

"I'll wait a few days, just in case."

David McCally was a transformed boy with his scrubbed face and new clothes. Mowrey even had him wearing boots and a hat. "Uncle Teddy, you and Aunt Mowrey going to buy a ranch in Montana and build a big house someday?"

Sandy frowned at Mowrey. "That what your Aunt Mowrey said?"

"She said someday you'd be a big rancher and I could have my very own horse," the boy said with glee.

"Well, I don't know about the ranch, but there's a big black horse down at the corrals that belongs to you right now."

Sandy decided to stay in Silver City a week. He had no desire to stumble onto Grandview, but he wanted to make sure he was long gone.

Silver City thrived on its namesake: *silver.* The desolate mountains of the Owyhee range in southwest Idaho supported only minimal life. Tons of supplies had to be freighted into the mountains every day. The price of everything almost doubled. During the week, Sandy, Mowrey, and David saw two melodramas, bought gifts for Bob Roy and Melissa, and lounged at the Idaho Hotel lobby. They even rode out to the Cosmos, Shoenbar, and Morning Star mines. They seldom ran into Mudd.

"Thompson," Mowrey said as they began to pack up the supplies, "I don't think Davy can ride a horse all the way to Montana. Perhaps we should buy a wagon."

"If he gets tired, he could double up with one of us. Do you know what they charge for a wagon here? It's outrageous. Besides, I'm not sure how we'd float it across the Snake."

Sandy led the horses around to the front of the hotel. He thought he needed only three pack-horses. However, after a study of the pile of baggage on the sidewalk, he knew they'd need more room. He just stared, muttered, and shook his head. Mudd drove up just then with the most interesting rig.

Mudd, with some friends, pulled a light freight wagon with five-foot-high wooden sides and a flat wooden roof. Wooden doors had been added in front and back. The sides were painted bright yellow with bold red letters: C. E. "Montana" Mudd: Traveling Mercantile & Ladies Emporium.

"Mudd! Where on earth did you—?"

"Ain't it a beauty?" Mudd beamed. "I figure I'll be a traveling merchant . . . you know, visiting ranches and the like. I always seen myself as a peddler. I got this rig and planned we'd tie those pack mules on to pull it. It cost a pretty penny, but ain't it worth it?"

"Mudd, every Indian and cutthroat within three hundred miles will see you coming."

"Exactly. And I'll have plenty of goods to sell 'em."

Sandy was considering whether this might be the time to end his limited partnership with Mudd when he caught Mowrey's imploring eye.

"Thompson, let him use the stock, and we can use the wagon for extra baggage. It will also give David a place to rest when he's tired."

David was already sitting on the seat of the gaudy wagon shouting, "Giddyap!"

After one last meal at the hotel, the party rode east out of Silver City. Sandy led, followed by Mudd and his wagon, with Mowrey and David riding horseback alongside. Day after day they journeyed across the plains up to the Oregon Trail and along the Snake. Mudd sold all his merchandise to the first couple of wagon trains of emigrants, but Sandy still couldn't help laughing whenever he saw Mudd's wagon. Its outline against the wilderness produced a stark picture of contradictions.

At Big Wood Creek they found an Irishman named O'Keefe who was building a huge raft to ferry settlers across the river to the northern trail. They waited two days for him to finish, then became his first customers. Sandy swam the stock across while Mowrey, David, Mudd, and the wagon ferried.

For the next six days there was no trail to follow. Then they got back to the main trail north to Montana. As much as Sandy had reminded them the wagon could entice Indian attacks, they saw no Indians at all. By the time they crossed Monida Pass they escaped immediate Indian danger. The nights grew colder, and the days shortened. Sandy recalled it had been a little over four months since he climbed off the train at Ogden. It seemed like a century ago.

They rode into Three Forks on a Saturday afternoon. Families lined the streets for weekly shopping. Cowhands hurried to spend their pay. Sandy pulled up in front of the sheriff's office and helped David down out of the wagon. They swung open the door to greet a somber Bob Roy. "Hey, you don't look so happy to see us," Sandy chided.

"Sorry about that. I've been tied up with some things since you've been gone. Just busywork. Come on, let's go see Melissa."

Bob Roy grabbed his hat and locked the door as they filed out. Sandy noticed he tossed his badge on the desk. Melissa was all smiles as she greeted them. As soon as their gear was unloaded, she and Mowrey looked through all the treasures they brought back. Mowrey showed off the silver and gold clock the trappers brought them.

David happily devoured a plate of oatmeal cookies and romped with Lucifer, the Wileys' yellow mutt.

"Bob Roy. . . Melissa," Sandy began. "I've got a big favor to ask. Until Mowrey and I can get a place of our own, David here needs a stable home. He's a good little fellow, and I'd be happy to help with the grub bill, but I would like you to consider caring for him awhile."

"We'd love to!" Melissa exclaimed.

"We can't," Bob Roy interrupted.

Melissa looked shocked. "Bob Roy, you didn't. . . ."

"There's no other way. Of course I did." Bob Roy turned to Sandy and Mowrey. "We'd be happy to have the boy, but things are pretty uncertain here. The city owns this house, and I've decided to quit the sheriff's job. I'm just not sure what'll be happening with us next."

"You got another job lined up?" Sandy inquired.

"No, that's the point. We've got some figuring to do."

"But why quit? You fit this job like a well-worn boot. And Melissa here's expecting any day. She has this place as neat as an Episcopal church!"

"Save your breath, Sandy," Melissa broke in. "I've tried to talk to him for a week. It's more complicated than that—"

"Melissa!" Bob Roy cut his wife short.

"Bob Roy Wiley, I don't understand. Sandy Thompson is your good friend. Surely you can talk it out with him."

"There's no talking left to do. I'm going to see the city council." He tramped out the door.

"Melissa, what's going on here? Is someone forcing him out?"

"Well, it's . . . I mean, I shouldn't, but. . . ." The lovely Southern smile vanished from her lips and eyes. "It's all George Whittley's doings. The newspaper story about you and Whittley made it back east somehow. Someone mailed a paper to the home folks. It must have gotten up to the Shenandoah, because two weeks ago Bob Roy received a telegram over in Bozeman ordering him to arrest you immediately so you could return to Virginia to stand trial. He decided to ignore the whole matter. Unfortunately, the telegraph operator's a relative of Whittley's. So, George stormed into his office last Saturday and demanded that Bob Roy arrest you the minute you hit town. He even riled up the mayor and city council. Bob Roy told them all he'd resign before he'd arrest a friend like you, and. . . ."

"And now I'm back."

"That's it, I'm sorry, Sandy."

Sandy ran after Bob Roy, although he didn't know what he'd say or do. He found him conversing with some men in front of the dry goods store. It turned out to be an ad hoc meeting of the city council. Bob Roy was about to turn away from the heated voices.

"Excuse me, gentlemen," Sandy interjected, "I'm Sandy Thompson and I've come to give myself up to the custody of your sheriff."

Bob Roy pulled him aside. "Save it, Sandy. They've already accepted my resignation."

"I know what I'm doing. Just follow me." Sandy turned back to the men on the sidewalk. "I'm sure that if I'm in the Three Forks jail, you fine men will give Bob Roy his job back . . . right?"

They agreed. In a matter of minutes Sandy sprawled in the tiny cell. Bob Roy sat in a chair on the other side of the iron. "Now, let's figure this thing out before anyone does something rash," Sandy began.

Bob Roy shot back. "Like giving in to Yankee justice?"

"Look, as long as I'm here in jail, Whittley can't complain and your job's secure. Let me see that telegram you got from Virginia."

He opened the upper right drawer of his desk and pulled out a much-folded message. Sandy gawked at the note. "I guess you never do outrun the past, no matter how far you go. Know who I saw in Silver City? Grandview! Millions of trails in this wide-open country, and I keep bumping into him. Now even telegrams hunt me down."

Bob Roy flopped down in his oak chair and exhaled slowly. "How about the whole gang of us moving to Arizona Territory? I hear they can use lots of help down in Lincoln County."

"I appreciate the offer, but I've got to settle up some of my accounts once and for all."

"You going back to Virginia?"

"I hope not. Let's try something different first. I took twelve hundred dollars from the mill. That's what they auctioned it for, and none of my family ever got paid. They wouldn't even listen to my case. How about you sending a wire to Bozeman, telling them I'll send the twelve hundred dollars plus three hundred dollars interest? Ask them if they still want me arrested under those conditions. If so, they should send you traveling expenses for my trip to Virginia. Then, send a duplicate copy to the president."

"Who?"

"President Grant. Oh, I know he probably gets thousands of such messages. But maybe a whole mess of them will convince him to halt the carpet-bagging system. In the meantime, I'll stay put in this jail if you'll bring me some books and some of Melissa's home cooking."

"What do you think they'll say?"

"Don't know. Figure I'll let them surprise me." Sandy lay back on the cot and closed his eyes.

It took over a month to hear from Virginia. Meanwhile, on November 4, 1870, William Theodore Wiley was born, and Whittley pressured the city council to send Thompson on without further instructions. He even offered to pay all expenses.

Sandy spent most his days reading in Bob Roy's office. His favorite was Washington Irving's account of *The Adventures of Captain Bonneville.* Most nights he walked the rounds with Bob Roy, who explained to anyone who asked, "I'm just exercising the prisoner." On more than one occasion he slipped into the back door of the Wiley house about dark and didn't return to the jail until daybreak.

Montana Mudd left Three Forks the day after the baby was born, loaded down with goods to sell to the miners of northern Idaho. He and Sandy tentatively made plans to meet again in Lewiston, Idaho, before December. Mowrey began to talk of a place on the Camas Prairie that would make a perfect ranch. She thought maybe the Nez Percé chiefs might let her have it.

On November 12, Sheriff Wiley received a long letter from Winchester, Virginia. The mill agreed to accept the money and drop the charges if Sandy would sign a quitclaim deed to the mill, which was enclosed.

Sandy hated to sign the note, but his chances of ever returning to Virginia and making any claims were so slim. At least that one episode could be solved. Bob Roy notified the city council. George Whittley was in Denver at the time, so they missed the satisfaction of knowing his response.

Sandy and friends celebrated that night at the Wiley house. "You know, I'm glad that's over. It's a big relief to me," Sandy told them all. "It's like the Lord's been nagging me about taking that money. Now maybe my life can ease up."

"Now Grandview won't have any reason to come after you either," Mowrey suggested.

"Trouble is, Grandview's not the type to need an excuse. It's personal with him. And I suppose he won't hear nor care about news from Virginia.

Someday, someplace, sometime, I'll face him again."

Melissa enrolled David in school. He was too young to attend officially, but they were short of students and agreed to take him. By now Melissa and Bob Roy were "aunt" and "uncle," too. David's favorite pal was his black horse, which he called Happy.

When Mowrey and Sandy talked of going to Idaho, Melissa put her foot down. "You're not taking David into the snows this time of year. Besides, he's in school, and he's a good helper. I need him. He gives Bob Roy someone to play with when I'm tied up with little William. You wouldn't be able to get back over the mountains until spring. I can't wait that long to see David. David will just have to stay. Isn't that right, Davy?"

"Yes, ma'am, I mean Aunt Melissa. I love it here." David had been well-groomed by his new aunt.

"Well, it does seem to be best for the time being, especially if Peter McCally should show. This is the closest thing David's had to a home in a long time." Sandy walked outside, with Mowrey close behind. They bundled in the frigid northern air and watched the sunset.

"We could wait until spring," Mowrey proposed. "I'm sure you could find work."

"It's not the work, Mowrey. I know this is really

hard, but it's something inside me that says it's time to move on. It's one of the reasons I hesitated about marriage. Call it nerves or the jitters, or just being restless."

"I call it Indian blood," Mowrey said with a smile. "I've heard about it my whole life. Is it because of Grandview? Is that why you can't stay in one place?"

He glanced to the northwest. "I don't think so. It's just that somewhere out there's a place that will feel like home to me. Somewhere I was meant to be. The old-timers in the Bible knew the feeling. 'Wandering Aramaeans' they called them. I just know I'll sense it when I see it. I think the Lord's starting to work things out—Darlene and David, the stolen mill money—but I haven't found my place yet."

"But what's wrong with Three Forks?" Mowrey ventured.

Sandy sighed. "Nothing. It's just not. . . ." He glanced to the northwest. "It's going to be cold up there."

"It will be warm at Lapwai. It's on the river. Lewiston, too. It's always mild in Lewiston. They even have fruit trees there."

By midmorning the next day they were on their way. They took only one packhorse with supplies, leaving their other possessions with the Wileys. Mowrey insisted on taking the gold and silver clock along. For the first time in several months,

Mowrey put on her buckskins again. She enjoyed the feel.

As they left Three Forks, Mrs. Madsen, who had the post office in her living room, met them in the middle of the street. "You be seeing Mr. Mudd?"

"We hope to." Sandy wondered what sort of trouble Mudd would be in by now.

"Give him this letter, please. It's been sitting here almost a month." She handed him an envelope from Sprinkle Hills, Illinois.

CHAPTER
13

Sandy and Mowrey rode west out of Three Forks, then climbed the grade through Pipestone Pass. They rimmed the timberline along the north slope of the Pioneer Mountains. Several nights they awoke to find snow on the ground. They followed Rock Creek north to the Clark Fork, then journeyed due west to the eastern entry of the Lolo trail.

Sixty-five years earlier Lewis and Clark had stood at the same place, Sandy reflected. *But, I think they must have come this way in the spring.*

Lolo Pass was one of the lower trails across the Bitterroot Mountains. But in late November, snow was everywhere. They had just passed the saddle of the Lolo, not quite to the Lochsa, when a fierce storm penned them in. Mowrey's tent wouldn't begin to hold against the blizzard, so Sandy left Mowrey huddled in a small stand of trees in search of shelter. He couldn't see more than a few feet.

In the side of the mountain he located a cave that would at least take the sting out of the blowing snow. He could even build a fire if they could find wood. He returned down the hill to the trees where he thought he had left Mowrey, but he couldn't find her. Yelling did no good. The storm's roar drowned out his voice and the bitter blast froze his lungs.

Mowrey crouched low against a tree, clenching a buffalo robe about her shoulders. She hadn't been this cold in a long time. She stared into the forlorn gray-white landscape, watching for any sign of Sandy. Life in the woods never panicked her—it was home. But the thought of losing Sandy frightened her. She always prided herself on her fierce independence. But deep down she had a strong desire to find security. And that was what Sandy provided.

Sandy wrapped his hands in bandanas while leading the horse through the deep drifts. He could see no more than five feet in front of him, but kept hoping to stumble onto some familiar landmark. Every few feet he studied the surroundings. Now he wasn't even sure he could find the cave again once he reached Mowrey. *Why did I go off on my own?* he berated himself.

His ears had long since passed the numb stage. Now his feet throbbed, for the leather on his boots was soaked clear through. He stumbled and fell and lay in the snow a moment. It felt warmer there than standing up, but anxiety for Mowrey drove him on.

Mowrey dug down to ground level and folded the large buffalo robe on the ground. Then she piled it high with snow. Next she climbed into the fold of the robe, shoving the snow up as she sat up. From the rear she looked like a snowdrift. From the front there was a tiny window where her face strained for a glimpse of Thompson. Meanwhile, the snow insulated her.

Sandy reached the frightening realization he might not find Mowrey. He had no idea which direction the trees would be from here. He decided he'd better circle back to the cave and try to warm up before he searched for Mowrey again. Now, could he find the cave?

In her rush to get out of the cold, Mowrey neglected to bring a gun into the buffalo hide. She hadn't counted on needing it. As she peered into the driving snow, a movement out of the trees from the north startled her. "Thompson!" she cried. Only a few steps away stood the biggest grizzly bear she'd ever seen. Her first reaction was to pull the robe down quickly over her head. The ploy worked. The snowdrift on her head and shoulders partially slid down the front part of the robe, entombing her in the snow. The bear lumbered after the horses instead, who broke free and scattered in their fear.

Sandy thought he heard a neigh. But when he stopped to listen, just the wind wailed. Still, he held out a hope. *Maybe Mowrey's looking for me.* As he plunged toward the direction of the sound, he floundered into the packhorse, then Mowrey's horse. He tied them to a tree, then pulled out his rifle and plowed into the horses' tracks, already fading.

The giant grizzly dug into the snowdrift that covered Mowrey. He'd given up on the horses and now pawed at the buried buffalo robe for the human prize. The bear's preoccupation aided Sandy. He could barely make out the familiar grove of trees and was almost on the bear before he saw it. The bear raised up, towering over Sandy, who fired a quick shot with his frigid hands. He only managed to catch the bear in the shoulder. The bear turned to leap at Sandy.

His second shot hit the bear in the throat, which infuriated the animal. Sandy tried to run, highstepping through the deep snow. He circled the stand of trees, trying to outdistance the bear enough to turn around and shoot. This time he pierced the lung with one shot and hit the bear's head with another. Yet, the massive beast hardly slowed down.

Sandy now groped near the snowdrift that the bear had been pawing. The huge animal lunged at him. As the claws ripped into Sandy's coat he jabbed the rifle barrel at the bear's open, bloody mouth and pulled the trigger. The bear collapsed on top of him. He would have been completely trapped had it not been for the rifle that propped up its head and shoulders.

A frightened, muffled voice startled Sandy. "Thompson!" He wrenched out from under the bear, and wildly looked around for Mowrey. "Get off me," she wailed. Her voice seemed to come from the direction of the bear.

Sandy yanked away the rifle and rolled the bear down the drift, then frantically dug in the snow. He soon found the buffalo hide and Mowrey. He hauled her out of the snow and they clung to each other for a long time.

Before dark they managed to find the horses and even locate the small cave. Mowrey started a fire.

"Did you worry about me?" she asked as they treasured the hot coffee they held.

"I sure did. I worried about me, too. I put five shots into that bear before he halted."

Mowrey shuddered. "You're lucky five shots brought him down."

"I've got to be grateful to that beast, though," Sandy added as he poured more coffee. "If he

238

hadn't been digging in the snow for you, I'd have passed you by."

He stared into the biting storm's horizontal pelting just a few feet away. "You want to hear something funny?" He turned to her robe-framed face, half-hidden in the flickering light. "My first thought when I heard you call out was that the bear had swallowed you. See what the cold does to your mind?"

Sandy's face softened into a pleased grin, but Mowrey only answered with a snore.

Sandy woke before dawn. The storm had subsided and the daylight revealed a crystal clear, frozen landscape. They hiked down to where they had tied the horses. They had survived the night by huddling together and kicking away the wolves. As they began to ride past the half-eaten corpse of the great grizzly, Mowrey dismounted and walked over to him.

"Mowrey! What are you doing?"

"It's an old Indian custom," she replied as she removed the bear's claws. Some of them looked to be over six inches long. "These will make a fine necklace."

"I didn't know you liked jewelry."

"Oh, it's not for me. It's for you," Mowrey informed him.

"But, I couldn't wear those—"

"Thompson, you'll wear them when you meet my people. Then they'll know how brave you are.

He who wears the claws of a grizzly is a strong warrior."

The further down the Lochsa they rode, the thinner the snow. At the Clearwater, only patches remained. At the junction of the south fork of the Clearwater, all snow disappeared. Here they came upon the first Indian encampment. Mowrey in her buckskins and Thompson with his claw necklace were immediately welcomed.

Mowrey didn't know any of the families on the south fork, but they did have mutual relatives. She spoke fluent Nez Percé and often stopped to translate for Sandy.

Many of the Indians spoke English taught to them by a mission school. They listened spellbound to Sandy's account of the grizzly encounter. When he finished, Mowrey chattered to them in Nez Percé. The whole clan burst into laughter as they slapped their legs.

"What did you tell them?" Sandy asked her.

"I told them the part about you thinking the grizzly swallowed me."

"And what did they say?"

"They said you must have confused me with Jonah. They remember the Bible stories well."

In three days they reached Lapwai and greeted more Nez Percé. Mowrey's Uncle Luke met them at Spaulding and took them up the valley to his small log house. They stayed several days there, with Mowrey catching up on the family news. Sandy tried to learn a few words in Nez Percé.

Mowrey told the tribal leaders about the meadow at the head of Lapwai Creek she hoped could provide a home for her and Sandy. They agreed that such a meadow would be a worthy place for a Nez Percé squaw and a warrior as brave as her husband. "It will be yours, Naw-too-pah, but never his. It's Nez Percé land forever."

Uncle Luke, his two sons, plus Mowrey and Sandy, decided to survey the meadow. The ascent up the Craig mountains was arduous. By the time they reached the high prairie at four thousand feet, six inches of light snow filled the countryside. To the east stretched the rolling prairie of scattered pines and numerous camas bushes. They rode into the forest of huge yellow ponderosa pines that dominated one hillside. Black pines, red firs, and an occasional spruce were scattered about. The tamaracks had long since turned yellow and lost most of their needles.

Sandy estimated the meadow to be about fifty acres, with timber covering the surrounding countryside. The idyllic meadow drained the spring runoff into Lapwai Creek.

Mowrey watched Sandy's face. "Didn't I say it would be a beautiful ranch site?"

"Ranch? Mowrey, this is timber country. It's a perfect place for a mill. See that hill to the east? We'll put our mill there, and we'll build a house in that draw. Or maybe on the hill, too. How about a house on a hill? Then we'll dam up the creek and fill the meadow for a log pond. Uncle Luke told us Lewiston's a growing town that needs lumber. You can't get lumber up to those gold mine towns fast enough. These yellow pines are just begging to be cut." Sandy rode over to investigate the trees a little closer. "Go ask your uncle what he thinks of the idea," he called out.

Mowrey caught up with him a little later. "He says he thinks the council will agree to the mill, provided you supply them with ten new houses each year. Uncle Luke wants the first one. And it has to have a floor."

The trip down the grade sped by. It was steep, but dry. Back, in Lapwai they made plans to begin work the following spring. Sandy knew he'd need some help, and lots of capital.

"I need a partner," he told Mowrey one night.

"You've got a partner, remember? He's in Lewiston."

"You mean Mudd?"

"I bet he could peddle every board you could cut."

The next morning Sandy rode alone to Lewiston. Lewiston was a river town located on the confluence of the Snake and Clearwater. It also served as an Indian settlement on the Nez Percé reservation. In addition, it was a merchant town which supplied such infamous gold fields as

Pierce, Florence, and Dixie. It was just the kind of place for such a one as Montana Mudd.

Sandy found Mudd at the Palouse Merchants Association arguing over the price of brass pans. Sandy slapped the trader on the back. "Mudd! I've been looking all over town for you. But I couldn't see that yellow wagon anywhere."

"Partner! You're just the one I wanted to see. With a little advice, and, uh, help, from you, I could corner the market on brass pans for the whole Northwest. What do ya think of that?"

So Mudd was busy organizing another vender's empire.

"Oh, about the wagon. . . . Well, I hate to admit it, but I got so tired of bumping along in the icy snow that I hacked her up and made a raft. Sold my horses to a trapper and floated the whole shot right down here to Lewiston. And listen to this—I had no more than tied her up to the dock when a family of Chinamen wanted to buy it. They floated it on down to the Columbia." Mudd motioned Sandy to follow him.

Out on the street Mudd asked, "Where's Mowrey?"

"Back in Lapwai with some of her relatives."

"And little David?"

"He's in Three Forks. Why?"

"Grandview's in town. Somehow he knows you're around and he's been trying to rile up folks against the Indians. Guess he figures you'd be out there with them. He's just actin' wild most of the time."

"Don't underestimate Grandview," Sandy warned. "He's shrewd."

When Sandy explained the opportunity at Lapai meadow, Mudd jumped at the offer. "Let's spend the winter raising the capital," Mudd suggested in a surprising moment of business acumen, then added, "after we settle with Grandview."

"Hey, are you Thompson?" A weak-eyed, bent, balding man hailed Sandy.

"Yes, I am." Sandy grimaced as he thought about how many people knew he was in town.

"There's a guy down at the Lazy 6 Saloon looking for you. You might want to get down there and have him a little talk. What he's tellin' folks about you ain't too neighborly."

"Montana, you stay out of this," Sandy began.

"What? The least you could do is buy a thirsty man a drink. Besides, I've got to be protectin' my future . . . partner."

Lewiston, Idaho, looked like dozens of other places in the West. Mainly new, unpainted buildings that had a habit of looking old after a single hard winter. Tent tops skirted the town, and the streets spread in general disarray. The Lazy 6 could have been the Lucky Strike in Dodge, the Silver Slipper in Virginia City, or the Golden Canary in Hangtown.

The two-story building spread twenty-five feet

wide and a hundred feet long. At the back stood a small stage for special performances. The west wall held a huge wooden bar, complete with brass rail under a fifty-foot mirror. It had been shipped around the Horn, and floated and portaged up the Columbia and Snake rivers. Dispersed along the center floor, and against the east scattered several dozen wooden tables and chairs. Private rooms filled the upstairs.

A dozen men or so leaned against the bar, tended by three men. At least twenty more men drank and gambled at the tables. Far from the door, near the stage, sat Robert Grandview.

Six men sat with him. He held a deck of cards, but no one played. All in the room had heard his earlier speech: "I've come to bring final justice to the war. I'm rounding up the cutthroats and thieves who escaped the South before the final surrender." He repeated the name Sandy Thompson often.

Before he entered the Lazy 6, Sandy checked the barrel of his pistols. He inserted another bullet. Sandy had never carried a full six bullets in his pistol. He had always left one chamber empty, and the hammer set on that chamber, to prevent an accidental shot in the leg. But now he loaded up. He also checked the twelve cartridge loops in the back of his belt. He carried a full load there, too. Knife hanging at his left hip, butt end forward, he strode in.

"Let me get situated first," Mudd said. "I want to have a good seat."

Sandy's eyes shot around the room. He spotted the back exit by the right side of the stage and decided to do his talking from the front door side of the long narrow room.

"That's the man I've told you about," Grandview railed. "Thompson is a Rebel thief and murderer. He's wanted in Virginia for robbery, and who knows what else. I say it ain't fair that good boys bled and died so that lawbreakers like him can go free."

Mudd quickly committed himself. "Ain't no truth to that robbery charge. The sheriff at Three Forks checked it all out."

Grandview pounded the table as he stood. "So he's got a friend. That don't mean he's not guilty. The very reason he's come to this room is to kill me. He don't like folks knowing the truth. Did I go out looking for him? No sir, he's on the prowl. And I think it's time he got some good Western justice. What do you say, boys?"

Sandy's eyes narrowed. "Grandview, if you have a beef with me, let's settle it outside."

"See? What did I tell you? Wants to bushwhack me. Some Reb moves in and thinks he can shoot anybody who knows what he's really like. Trying to make us all sitting ducks." Grandview's eyes and mouth twitched with indignation.

"You're in a lot of trouble, boy," a burly man at

the bar sneered. He rested his right hand on a white-shanked Colt. A few others took a stance before Sandy. Several got up to leave. Some backed into the corners.

Sandy quickly sized up the ones who faced him. He decided no more than three would actually draw their guns. Three, and Grandview. "Fellas," he stalled, "I don't know a one of you, but I'm guessing you know each other. The first one who draws insures that one of your wives will be a widow, or a mother loses a son. I might not be fast enough to stop all of you, but I figure I can get three to four shots before I'm down. To be honest, I just don't miss at this range.

"The first shot will hit the talkative fellow at the bar. The second will slam the upper chest of Grandview. The third'll hit the fellow in the black hat next to Grandview. A big head like that should make an easy target. If I happen to get a fourth bullet, it'll go to the nervous fellow leaning against the wall, sliding his hand toward his gun. Now, which of you wants to get this thing rolling?"

Sandy's speech caught them all by surprise. Several more rose up and tried to back out. The three bartenders fidgeted. One of them exited to the upstairs rooms. Sandy surmised this last group of men wouldn't desert Grandview. They could be on a payroll, or too hungry for a fight to back out. But in a game of seconds, any doubts he could cast would be to his advantage.

"Sandy! Behind you!" Mudd screamed out, then he was stopped by a smashing right by one of the men from the bar. Another man followed up with another slug to his middle.

Sandy turned to draw on someone who had faked leaving the room. He caught a wooden chair across his right arm. His gun spun across the room. He flung the chair out of the man's arm and buried his right fist deep in the man's stomach. Then he brought up his right knee with a resounding crack. The man collapsed, but Sandy was far from safe.

The others moved in with chairs swinging. Sandy dove under the blow of the first one, butting the man hard with his head. Sandy's hat flew off, but the man was down. Sandy rolled off the man so fast that a second chair missed him completely and shattered instead across the downed man's chest.

Sandy took a blow to the upper body that glanced off, then one to the jaw that didn't. He slammed several hard punches at any target he could reach, causing men to stumble back in all directions. There was a hard blow on his right side, about the kidney, that caused him to lurch. Then a large man caught him with a powerful uppercut.

Blood poured from Sandy's mouth. He sprawled across a table as the big man charged in for another blow. The heel of Sandy's boot caught the man with frightful impact in the Adam's apple. The man slumped to the floor, gasping for air.

The split-second pause gave Sandy a chance to dive for his gun. It had landed at the base of the bar. The nervous man against the east wall now drew his gun. His shot missed by three feet.

Sandy's didn't. The bullet caught the man's right shoulder and slammed the man against the wall, forcing him into a sitting position. Sandy rolled behind the mahogany bar and fired one more shot that splintered the table behind which Grandview ducked. Everyone now found cover, guns drawn.

Six gunmen surrounded him. He pumped two more cartridges into the empty chambers and waited. Breaking glass gave the first clue. Sandy sped down to the opposite end of the bar. The man with the black hat who'd been standing next to Grandview had crawled there, too. He inched around the polished wood and poked his nose around for a peek. He stared into the barrel of Sandy's Confederate pistol less than two inches away from his left eye.

Sandy crashed the pistol's barrel against his skull. The man's head thudded to the floor.

Meanwhile, Grandview dove for an open shot from the north end of the bar. Sandy glimpsed the smoke from the gun as he felt lead burn high in his right leg. With great effort, he pulled himself around the end of the giant bar.

Sandy returned Grandview's fire from this poor position. All he heard was the jangled sound of shattering glass. The click of a hammer cock spun him around. For a moment he glared at a pistol held at point-blank range. Before he had time to react, a bowie knife flew from out of nowhere, slicing deep into the fleshy part of the man's upper arm. He dropped his gun.

Mudd's in the battle! Sandy cheered silently.

But a blow to the back of the head with a brass spitoon felled Mudd. Four gunmen remained in fighting condition. Sandy filled the empty chambers of his gun again. He barraged them with a burst of fire and plunged behind the curtain of the stage. A dozen shots treaded on his heels, but Sandy rolled clear to the east side of the stage. His leg seethed as he tore off his shirt to tie around the wound. The bullet had passed clean through the leg.

Sandy could hold them off a little longer, but he only had ten bullets left. What he wanted more than anything was a clear shot at Grandview.

Sandy whirled when he thought he saw the curtain move. He fired a shot through the heavy green velvet. A man fell motionless on the front of the stage.

He examined the stage area from his guarded position. Several sets of curtains hung high above him. The backdrop on the rear wall was freshly painted and there were several small doors on the opposite side of the stage. He deduced they were either exits or stairways to the top of the curtains. He considered climbing up to those curtains. If Grandview and the others charged in, he'd make a better angle.

Before he could make a move, he heard noise on the stage front. He fired another shot through the curtain that thudded against wood. *They've shoved a table up on the stage!* Sandy determined.

Sandy fired a couple of quick shots at the huge pullies above the velvet curtain. The curtain dropped on three men behind the table. One attempted to retreat and tripped in the grips of the heavy curtain. Sandy's shot knocked his legs out from under him. Grandview and the last gunman tore out. At last, Sandy had his open shot.

His pistol clicked empty.

He raced to cram in his last five bullets. With the main curtain draped across the table, Sandy's position was exposed. He made a break for the stairs. He immediately fell on his face when he put weight on his wounded leg. This caused him to miss being hit by a bullet intended for him. Hidden from sight by the table and curtain, he rolled to the other side of the stage. The gunman who had fired the shot raised up to investigate. He took a shot in his left shoulder blade.

The bodies splayed around the room reminded Sandy of the war. But, he didn't have much time for contemplation. The door he assumed led to the stairs was locked. He threw his weight against it and ripped the safety bolt. It wasn't the door to the stairs.

Ginny McLain hated Lewiston, Idaho. She preferred San Francisco, or Denver, or even Spokane. Adler's Gulch would beat playing in a town like Lewiston. Ginny was pretty, but not gorgeous. She could sing well, but she wasn't spellbinding. She knew some influential people, but they weren't quite important enough. As a result, the pride of Independence, Missouri, as she considered herself, was stuck in places like Lewiston. *And not even the main hotel,* she thought.

She'd come to the saloon an hour early to practice, but couldn't find the piano player. Since the men out front appeared to be in a fighting mood, she didn't want to be around them. So she retreated to the tiny dressing room to change clothes and put on makeup. She was peering into a dirty, cracked mirror when she heard the shooting begin. When the shooting came closer, Ginny nearly collapsed. She was accustomed to fighting off the advances of drunken cowboys, but this was different. She probed the cramped, dark quarters for a weapon. The only thing she could find was a set of Indian clubs perched in one corner. She grabbed a blue striped one and raised it above her head in anticipation of an intruder.

Sandy never discovered if there was a stairway to the curtains or not. The club found its mark, and he was out before his body hit the floor.

CHAPTER
14

Some people say unconscious humans don't dream. Sandy did. He had visions of rolling pastures, stately homes, powerful racing horses . . . and flowers—violets, yellows, blues, and whites. Surely it was heaven, or Virginia.

Reality crept into the recesses of his memory. He ached from head to toe. He was strapped across his saddle, and his shirt was still tied around his wounded leg. The pain in his head was so great he wished he could pass out again, but that pleasure evaded him.

From this angle Sandy couldn't understand what was going on. He recognized a sunset, and men rode alongside and behind. He could see his horse being led by a man with a bandaged arm. The surrounding hills outside Lewiston loomed in the distance, as did the blurred silhouette of trees.

Just as his head felt like it would split open, the riders halted. They untied his feet and righted him in the saddle. Sandy noticed several of the riders were bandaged. He concluded he may have been responsible. Grandview supervised the action.

"Glad you could join us for the party, Thompson," he sneered. "Never did like hanging an unconscious man. Sort of dulls the festivities, if you know what I mean." He looked full in Sandy's face, so close Sandy could smell his foul breath, and he continued in a low voice only Sandy could hear. "Boy, don't you ever think for a moment you're going to pull something over on Robert Grandview. You're not the first Confederate scum I've tracked down, and hung. You're just the last. You're going to wish you died there at Fort Edwards."

As Sandy's mind cleared momentarily, he blurted out, "You men know it's Western courtesy to give a man a chance to say a few last words. Grandview, being from the East, doesn't understand that."

"You had your say!" Grandview bawled. "Yank that noose!"

"Leave him be," said a man in the front.

Sandy continued. "I'm assuming none of you boys fought for the Confederacy. But I would venture that several of you fought for Union troops. Did any of you ever hear of Fort Edwards? It was one of your forts in southern Ohio."

"Yeah, I heard of it," said a tall, thin man who inched his horse nearer.

A couple more nodded their heads.

"Did you ever hear anything good about Fort Edwards? Did you ever hear something that made you proud they were on your side? Well, did you?" Sandy's face perspired even in the cold dusk. His leg throbbed, but his mind fought for reason.

"Heard it was a hellhole," the thin man replied.

"I heard they killed all their prisoners," another man recalled.

"Well, they didn't kill them all," Sandy announced. All through his discourse Sandy scanned the horizon looking for signs of Mudd— or anyone. He was all alone.

"Let me tell you about some that died at Fort Edwards. Clement Smith was a sixty-one-year-old mountaineer from Tennessee. He wasn't even in the army. He—"

"We don't have to listen to these Rebel lies," Grandview growled, reaching for his gun. A rifle barrel in his ribs silenced him.

"He ain't going nowhere, Grandview. Let him finish. I got kinfolk back in Tennessee."

Sandy hoped he wouldn't pass out. He mustered enough strength to continue the story. "Clement Smith had two thousand head of hogs back in the hills. When Union troops claimed them for their breakfast, Clement fired warning shots. For that, they locked him in a prisoner of war camp. Well, the commander at Fort Edwards was trying to be a general. He figured if he got some of the prisoners to spill the beans on their buddies, he'd have secrets to pass on to the secretary of war, and thereby promote himself. So he called us all out in the hot sun one day for inspection and told us it was time for interrogation.

"Now, for some reason he started with old Clement. Maybe he looked the easiest to break. He asked him all sorts of questions about troop movements and such. Poor old Clement didn't know about anything except hogs. So the commander devised a means of persuasion. He tied Clement's hands to a table and chopped off his fingers, one at a time. We were all forced to watch and listen to the screams. Some of the boys fainted, and a good many lost their breakfast right in the yard."

"It's all a lie!" Grandview raged. "Clement Smith died trying to escape. It's all in the official reports."

"He died trying to escape, all right," Sandy affirmed. "By the time the commander finished with Clement's fingers and toes, the old man was delirious with pain. Somehow he pushed the guard aside and hobbled toward the camp gate. The commander personally shot him in the back. And I presume you all know that your friend, Grandview here, was the commander of that fort." Sandy tried to close his eyes a moment.

"That's enough!" Grandview charged. "This man, Thompson, is a dangerous criminal. Let's get on with it!" But Grandview had no listeners this time.

Sandy took a painful breath and rambled on. "Did you hear about Sherman Rangle? He was tied hand and foot and thrown in the river. Or Casey Natalie, tied to a stake and whipped to death. Or even Mallory Johnston, who lasted six days in the snow without even a shirt on his back. You picked a great partner in this man, Grandview. I didn't even tell you about my scar. It's twenty-seven inches long. I know, because with my hands tied above my head Grandview made those cuts one inch at a time. When the war was over, I testified against him. He was supposed to be put away for a long time. How he got out here I don't know."

"My God, men," Grandview shouted. "You can't believe a man when he's this desperate. I ran an efficient camp for the glorious cause of the Union."

"Ain't what I heard about Fort Edwards," the thin man interjected. "I heard that story about old man Smith once before."

Sandy's eyes scanned the horizon as he summed up his appeal. "What I ask of you is this. Let me and Grandview settle this, once and for all. Just the two of us, head to head. Out west here you men are noted for giving a man a fair chance to prove himself. What I'd like right now is a fair chance. And if you don't think I deserve one, how about giving me one for old Clement Smith and the others? They didn't even have the fortune of dying with honor. Just cut my ropes, toss me a pistol, and move out of the way."

Grandview panicked. "That's crazy! Let's get this hanging over. Remember, I'm buying all the drinks tonight."

The men began to murmur among themselves. "I never did like hangin's," one of them said. "Shoot-outs are better."

"Give the man his gun," another shouted.

"You can't do this! Don't you remember what he did back at the Lazy 6? This man's a thief and killer. He can't be trusted." Grandview had the strange sensation of losing control of the situation and of himself.

The man who Sandy recognized as the one who threw the first swing at him drew forward. "Well, Grandview, the way I see it, Thompson here purposely walked into that ambush back at the Lazy 6, and almost fought his way out of it. I got my shoulder banged up bad, but it was my own fault. Out here we just leave a man's past alone. We like to give him a new start, to see how he does. Seems to me you've both said a lot about the other. So, let's forget the past. If you two got a score to settle, I'd be happy to be a witness."

The man with the rifle in Grandview's side didn't back away as another rider circled behind Sandy and cut the ropes. Sandy rubbed his wrists, hoping for quick circulation. Another man jammed Sandy's pistol back into his holster, but kept his own pistol drawn. "Wouldn't want you havin' a head start," he explained.

All the riders, except the two holding guns on Thompson and Grandview, backed away. Finally, the last two sped off.

Sandy had always been confident he could out-draw any opponent. But right now was different. His body felt the effects of the violence he'd suffered the past few hours. And he had no idea about the cartridges in his gun. Did the other men empty it? Or did they spin the chambers and leave him with empty fire? He waited for Grandview to make the first move.

He fought for control of his mind. Old hatreds battled for dominance. Flashbacks of battles, stockades, and gory deaths attacked his reason, but he tried to master his reflexes. It took every ounce of energy left him to concentrate on Grandview and the guns.

Neither he nor the others noticed the fifty Nez Percé and Montana Mudd cresting the hill to quietly watch the proceedings.

For Robert Grandview, the death of Sandy Thompson would mean the end of an era, a time for new beginnings in a country made for men of big dreams and great ambitions. With a far-off smile on his face, he drew his pistol and fired.

The shot missed. At that moment Sandy had leaned low to the right of his horse and clutched the animal's neck with his left hand. From that angle he fired and caught Grandview in the left shoulder. Grandview tumbled from his horse.

Sandy scooted to the ground and pounced on Grandview before the wounded man could pass his pistol from the left hand to the right. He landed a hard right on Grandview's jaw. Grandview sprawled on his back, and Sandy's leg collapsed under him.

As Sandy used both hands to push himself back up from the ground, Grandview surprised everyone by pulling a knife from his boot. The blade flew through the air. Sandy jerked away, but the shining steel caught his right shoulder. Sandy slumped to his knees. He reached across with his left hand and tried to pull out the knife. He thought he heard Mowrey scream.

The riders from Lewiston turned to stare at the armed Nez Percé behind them. Grandview grabbed in the dirt for his pistol as Sandy rose to his feet, leaving the blade buried where it was. Blood poured down his unshirted back as he placed his gun in his left hand. He lunged for the spraddled Grandview just as his hand touched his weapon. Sandy's boot heel ground into Grandview's fingers. "Stand up, Grandview! I said, stand up!"

The tone of Sandy's voice brought terror to the seasoned army man. Sandy rocked on his feet, fighting to stay conscious.

Grandview slowly rose, and gasped for breath.

"Look, Thompson, you beat me. So I go my way and you go yours. My God, man, you can't shoot me now. Surely you men won't. . . ." He appealed to the riders, but they weren't about to pull guns while surrounded by Nez Percé. "Come on, Thompson, you've gotten even," he pleaded wildly.

"Even?" Sandy gasped for breath, as the pain in his shoulder was close to unbearable. *"Even?* How about old Clement Smith? Clement didn't have a chance to get even, did he?" Sandy whipped the gun barrel against Grandview's head. He fell back to the ground, clutching his new wound. Sandy could tell the knife in his back was doing its job. He was about to black out, and he couldn't tell if he was shouting or whispering. "And how about Casey and Mallory!" Grandview tried to rise to his feet but Sandy put the heel of his boot against the man's neck and shoved him back to the ground.

"How about the eighty-three who were blindfolded and shot after the war was over? How about it, Grandview? Did they get even?" He cocked the hammer back on the pistol. Grandview turned ghostly white.

From up on the hill Mudd stood up in the stirrups to see what would happen next.

Mowrey started to close her eyes, then she yelled. "Draw the line, Thompson. Remember? We'll tame this land. For God's sake, *draw the line!*"

She hid her eyes as she heard three shots ring out. Each shot tore away at her heart. *Why did he have to shoot him so many times?* She looked up in time to see Sandy fire the last two shots into the ground next to the cowering Grandview. She looked at Mudd, who nodded, "Yup, every shot went into the ground."

Mowrey slid off her horse and starting running to Sandy. He had slumped to his knees and was using the barrel of his pistol to draw a line in the dirt between himself and the wounded Grandview.

Grandview crawled toward his pistol, but the smash of a rifle barrel across his back flattened him in the dirt. The men from Lewiston were not going to let him shoot anyone else.

Sandy heard Mowrey talking to him. He could feel her by his side, but her voice sounded miles and miles away.

"Thompson, I was afraid you would kill him— and I was afraid you wouldn't." Mowrey sobbed.

Mudd was there now, pulling the knife from his back.

"Mowrey!" Sandy groaned.

She clutched his hand.

"Mowrey! You tell them," he grasped for air. "You tell them I drew the line. Lord knows, I drew the line." He slumped into her arms.

Sandy slept for three days at Uncle Luke's cabin. A root application relieved a leg infection and reduced a raging high fever. Neither the leg wound nor the knife wound was as critical as it could have been, but he'd lost a lot of blood. Mowrey now had a chance to do something she was very good at—taking care of her man.

After Sandy began to think clearly again, he suddenly remembered Mudd's letter. Mudd tore it open and read aloud:

July 27, 1870
Dear Clarence:
Since it has been some time since I heard from you (fourteen years to be exact), I am taking the liberty to mail a duplicate copy to each known address I have of yours. Therefore, I do not know if this will reach you in Rock Springs, Ogden, Laramie, Bozeman, Three Forks, or Mudd City.

When you left southern Illinois twenty-five years ago you said you would return. I believed you then. I still do. But if you recall, my father chased you off the porch with a shotgun and said it would be over his dead body that he would let me marry a Mudd. You might also remember that you remarked that it might just be over his dead body that you'd return.

I am writing to inform you that my father, Mr. Primsley, passed away yesterday after-noon at 3:36 p.m.

> *Still sincerely yours,*
> *Miss Eunice Primsley*
> *Sprinkle Hills, Illinois*

Mudd whooped and danced around. "She's mine, all mine!" He waved the letter and ran outside calling to every Indian he could find. "She's mine! Miss Eunice is mine!"

When the dust settled, Mudd left immediately for Lewiston. It was too far into winter to cross the mountains on horseback, so he booked passage on a boat down to Astoria. From there he would sail to San Francisco, then catch the transcontinental train. He planned to bring the new Mrs. Mudd west in the spring to join Mowrey and Sandy in setting up the lumber mill. "But I haven't even gotten to see the site," he wailed, "so I can tell Miss Primsley all about it."

Sandy wanted to see the meadow again. "Just once more before heavy winter sets in," he told Mowrey. "I'll have a better idea of the men and equipment I'll need in the spring."

The Indian leaders at Lapwai accepted Sandy's proposal to timber off the logs. They only insisted on one change. Uncle Luke explained, "The elders feel it necessary to mention Mowrey in the name of the company, since it's actually her ground."

Sandy nodded. "Well, then, instead of Thompson & Mudd, we'll call it Thompson, Mudd, & Mowrey."

"Oh, no, that won't do," Uncle Luke responded. "They'll only accept Mowrey, Thompson, & Mudd."

Mowrey laughed out loud when she heard about

it. Though Sandy wondered how much of this had been her doing, neither he nor Mudd objected to the name change.

Montana decided to leave for Illinois on December 30. He wanted to spend Christmas with Sandy and Mowrey. On December 23 a chinook swept into northern Idaho. The temperature went up forty degrees in less than two hours. As the snow melted, Sandy grew restless with cabin fever. He consulted Uncle Luke about taking the trip to the top of the mountain once more. "The Lapwai Creek grade would be hard to climb. You might go around by Waha, but that takes a lot longer. The trouble is, when this chinook ends, it will freeze again. It's a dangerous trip."

Sandy had little trouble convincing Mudd, who now spent his days pining for Miss Primsley. Mowrey expressed concern for Sandy's strength, then insisted on coming along.

On the morning of December 24 the temperature rose above sixty degrees in Lapwai. As the trio trekked up the canyon, they followed the creek brimmed with snow melt. The climb exhilarated them and the sun stood high in the heavens as they reached the meadow. Even an experienced traveler like Mudd marveled at the large yellow pines in the virgin forest. "I don't know if'n we can make any money up here, but it's the kind of place that makes a fellow want to settle down and live forever," he announced.

Sandy and Mudd stepped off distances and recorded them. In the spring Sandy would explore the best route to the top of the mountains. They could spend the early months road building. The Indians had told him of a nice grade at the end of Mission Creek. He wanted to try that next. If they were short of capital, they could cut timber and sled it down to Spaulding, then float the logs to the Clearwater in Lewiston.

Once they had money in hand, they'd get a big saw running. "And the prairie beyond the forest is just crying for cattle. Maybe not a fortune, Mudd, but enough for peace and a little security."

Mowrey prepared the fire for lunch on the north edge of the meadow. Brilliant white patches of melting snow littered the prairie. But before they'd finished eating, they sensed a change in the weather. Within an hour the temperature dropped from fifty to twenty-five degrees. Dark clouds rolled in, stacking up against the bitterroots. "Here it comes," warned Mowrey. "Just like Uncle Luke said."

They crept close to the fire while packing their horses. Mudd suggested they find shelter and sit it out until morning, but Mowrey and Sandy both wanted to get down the hill as far as they could.

"It drops three thousand feet down that canyon. We could get below snow level before dark," Sandy commented.

It was a difficult journey down the rocky slopes

of Lapwai Creek in the best of conditions. This was among the worst. The creek and its tributary streams ran wild. Much of the water began to ice. Waterfalls froze. Every slick boulder provided potential disaster.

They picked their way down the slope, often walking the horses. When they'd gone about four hundred feet, the snow hit. They could barely see, and Sandy kept his mind on the future sawmill as they trudged along.

Suddenly, Mowrey's cries pierced the stormy air. Sandy turned in time to see her horse hit the ground, and her, too. Its hind legs slid down the icy wall and into the creek below. Mowrey landed ten feet down the hill on her back. "It's broken! It's broken!" Mowrey screamed.

Thompson flew off his horse and stumbled down the cliff. His slick leather boots slid from rock to rock until he literally bounced along to the creek bed. "Lord, O Lord, please . . . no," he breathed as he reached his wife.

"It's broken, Sandy! I know it's broken." It was the first time she'd ever used his first name.

"What is it? Your leg?" He wiped away the fallen snow from her face and gently cradled her.

She sat up. "No, it's the clock. Our clock! I had it in the saddlebag. Now I know it's ruined." She pointed to where the now crippled horse lay panting on the rocks.

Sandy stared at the horse and then back to

Mowrey. "The clock? All this screaming about a clock?" He dropped her head back into the snow. "Come on, let's get out of this mess."

Sandy and Mudd stripped the gear off the horse while Mowrey waited on the trail. The snow almost blinded them as they hiked back up. "The clock—can it be fixed?" she asked anxiously.

"No problem. It's not even scratched. That's more than I can say for your horse," Sandy added.

"You didn't shoot him, did you?"

"We couldn't get him up this rocky slope. But maybe he can wander out on his own. At least he's got a fighting chance at it."

Sandy loaded Mowrey on his horse and climbed up behind her. Mowrey clutched the clock in her arms all the way back to her Uncle Luke's. As soon as she spotted a flickering kerosene light at the cabin, she looked down at the clock. "Look, it's ten minutes to midnight. We made it home before Christmas!"

Melissa Lindsay Wiley published her journals of life in the West in 1917. They were instant best-sellers. She died in 1929 at Denver, Colorado.

Bob Roy Wiley was fatally shot in the back in Billings, Montana, on July 16, 1891, by Dirty Pete Rogers of the Hole-in-the-Wall gang. Dirty Pete was hanged for the crime.

Robert Grandview survived his wounds and served sixteen years in prison at Fort Leavenworth, Kansas. He was hanged in Ensenada, Mexico, April 2, 1893, convicted of leading an army of 120 men in the invasion of Baja, California. The attempt to establish an independent country failed.

Clarence Earl "Montana" Mudd died in the Old Soldiers Home, Santa Monica, California, June 14, 1902.

David McCally became a noted trial lawyer in western Montana. He served as a state senator from 1898 until 1924. He was unsuccessful in his attempt to be elected governor in 1914. He died on his ranch near Three Forks, Montana, December 30, 1936. The whole state mourned his death.

Theodore Arthur "Sandy" Thompson and Mowrey Thompson led active, full lives. Their adventures and exploits are still recalled in rural homes of northern Idaho and western Montana. These accounts are also amply told in many publications. Most of the stories are true. The ornate clock given to the Thompsons in 1870 as a wedding gift is now housed in the Winchester Historical Museum, Winchester, Idaho.

Center Point Publishing

600 Brooks Road • PO Box 1
Thorndike ME 04986-0001 USA

(207) 568-3717

**US & Canada:
1 800 929-9108**
www.centerpointlargeprint.com